Key 13

Key 13:

And Other Stories

Rose Titus

Key 13: And Other Stories

Edited by Kelly Novak
Hypothesis Press
Andover, MA
www.HypothesisPress.com

ISBN-13: 9780999035719
ISBN-10: 0999035711

Contents

"Key 13" Or, a Visit to the Morgue!

When I was nineteen, one of my first jobs was as a nurse's aide. I first worked at a nursing home, the type of which is inhabited by elderly and handicapped people suffering from various sad ailments including dementia and worse. I am sad to say I often went home and cried as my car pulled up into my driveway. Perhaps the saddest part of working in the nursing home was that a large percentage of the other staff was of the type that, quite frankly, didn't give a damn about the comfort of the elderly in their last years. Stealing from patients, neglect, verbal abuse, and worse, was not uncommon. If one tried to report things, one could find one's tires slashed.

Because of that, and because they paid so little, after about a year and a half I went to work at a state hospital. I shall not name this state hospital, so as to not give it a worse reputation than it already has. The state hospital, despite having an unclean reputation, was a far, far better place for a disabled person to exist than the run for profit nursing home. The much older building was cleaner— except for a few cockroaches—almost odor free, and more importantly, I found that most, but certainly not all, of the staff were relatively decent people.

The state hospital held a variety of physically and mentally disabled patients, and many were extremely sad cases. There was one who had been homeless, living under a bridge due to mental illness, and now he was confined to a wheelchair and only able to say a few words. Although he now had nothing but the faded "johnny" he wore along with the socks on his feet, he did get a clean bed and three decent meals a day. The staff treated him kindly, although, like many patients, he was given a humorous nickname. In other words, the poor guy was lucky to be there. And since he could only manage a few words, each and every time he was approached by staff, he would declare, "No money! I don't got no money!" And so we called him, "Mr. No Money!"

There was also the sometimes pleasant, but more often downright scary, schizophrenic who, I was told, tried to ax murder his parents. He tried to escape once, but could not find his way out on his own, and we didn't help him. So, he stayed.

Then there was the even scarier violent mental patient who called everyone he saw by the "N-word," even if you were white.

There was the insane blind man who always wanted to kill me, even though I was nice to him. He kept trying to strangle me, screaming, "I'm going to kill you! I'm going to break your f---ing neck!" I had to get close enough to spoon feed him, however, so I needed to think of a way to keep him from killing me. There was always a cart filled with sheets and pillowcases, so I wrapped up a sheet tightly into the shape of what my neck might feel like, and said, "Mr. Smith, do you want to kill me?" "Yes! I want to kill you!" "Okay, want to break my neck?" "Yes, I want to break your f---ing neck!" "Okay, here's my neck! Squeeze real hard!" He seized the wrapped up bed sheet and began to strangle it with all his might. I got the chocolate pudding off his dinner tray and spoon-fed him that while he was attempting to kill me. I remember, he always ate well, whether he was trying to kill me or not.

There was the lady who constantly screamed about "the Devil!" whenever she was approached, and seemed downright possessed, although I have no proof that she was. I never saw her levitate, but if she did, I would be out of there fast.

Another lady was over six feet tall and appeared to be over three hundred pounds. She would come into the break room when I was trying to eat my lunch and try to steal my sandwich.

We wore white uniforms but they were soiled by the end of the day. Patients would frequently throw feces, vomit, or food at staff. Once again, a bed sheet would come in handy. If you knew a patient was going to throw feces at you, you could wrap the bed sheet around yourself like a big apron, then send it away with the rest of the laundry.

Once again, not all of the staff were morally upright. One was rumored to sell drugs. He had an expensive leather jacket and drove a Trans Am—on an orderly's salary. And another orderly, the young female staff was warned by older female staff, "Don't be in a room alone with him, and don't get on an elevator with him."

Older staff taught younger staff who to watch out for, for which I was grateful.

A staff member I will always remember was Doris— she thought of herself as a comedian. Although she was a well-meaning person, she could tire you out with her antics. Doris was about 40, but sometimes acted like an overgrown teenager.

One day Doris found out that the old hospital building did in fact have a morgue on the lower level. This got Doris all excited and she wanted to visit the morgue just to see what it was like down there. Naturally, I had to go to. I don't know why I felt I had to go to the morgue. Just to be brave, I suppose.

Doris went to find Agnes who of course was the oldest staff person in our ward. Agnes had probably worked at the state hospital the longest of anyone. She knew her way around. You could really learn a lot from a co-worker like Agnes. One of the best pieces of advice Agnes gave me the first day I started; she was taking me up to the floor where I would be permanently assigned, and said, "Now listen, in this place, you keep your eyes and ears open, and your mouth shut." And she was right. This advice can apply to a lot of workplaces, I suppose.

But on this day, Doris went to pester Agnes about letting us visit the morgue . . .

"Oh come on, can we, please?"

Agnes frowned at Doris, which was not unusual, as she generally frowned at everyone. *"You want to what?"*

"Go to the morgue!" Doris grinned like a big kid and pointed at me, "Rose wants to go!"

Thanks, Dorrie, "Yeah. Okay. If you guys go, I'll go along too . . . I guess."

Agnes frowned again, "Okay, but you two better keep it shut about this, you hear me! We are not supposed to be down there, so you both keep quiet."

"We promise," I said.

But Doris kept giggling.

The tree of us went down the elevator together. It dawned on me that maybe Doris wanted to see the two headed baby that was supposedly kept down there. Yes, that's right. A state hospital is a place filled with strange things. I learned that pretty quickly, and one of those

4

strange things was a two headed fetus that they say was stillborn and preserved in a glass jar.

At the turn of the century—I had learned while working there—the state hospital was a hospital for the poor. At that time, there was a maternity ward. That's how the two headed baby got there, that is what was said about it—that the sad creature had been born there and didn't survive, or was stillborn.

Now Doris is nudging me, "There's a two headed baby down there, you know."

"Yeah, I heard."

Agnes gave us another look, "Don't you two never say nuthin!"

"I promise," I said, and I meant it.

"Nuthin!" repeated Agnes.

She led us to the reception area, and asked for "Key 13." I didn't say anything, but I thought to myself, well, the people who run this crazy dump have a sense of humor, at least.

We followed her down the dark hall, and she opened the door to the morgue, and flipped on the lights.

It wasn't dark or cold, the way you would expect a morgue to be. It was well lit, clean, and the temperature was rather comfortable, no different from the atmosphere in the rest of the building. There were several drawers, of course, which were there to contain the departed. Doris began pulling them out, one after the other, but they were empty.

"Dorrie, will yah cut it out? It's disrespectful."

She laughed, "There ain't nobody in . . . whoa!"

The last drawer she pulled out contained a body. We did not see the entire body, just two large, cold dead feet.

5

She stopped pulling the drawer open when she saw it. She stopped suddenly and remained coldly still, looking down at the dead man's feet.

"Put that back, shut it, will yah?" I said.

And she did.

Agnes was finally smiling, "And there, on that shelf, is the two headed baby."

Yes, there it certainly was, contained in a glass jar. It was rather small, of course, possibly a conjoined twin of some kind that did not survive. I stared at it quietly, and hoped it didn't suffer for the short time that it had been alive. I wondered about the mother, also. Did they even tell her, back then, of the condition of her child? Perhaps not, if they were humane. I imagined they would have said, simply, the child was stillborn. And told her nothing else.

Next to the two headed baby was a glass jar filled with snakes.

"Agnes, why are there snakes in here? I get it about the two headed baby, being a unique specimen, and all—"

"They keep these things for the nursing students," she said. "To show them things like this."

"But why the snakes?"

"Maybe so the students can learn about things that can kill people." Probably she didn't really know, either.

Both the two headed fetus and the snakes were quite horrible to look at. I continued to stare at the glass jars. Suddenly, something grabbed me from behind—

I screamed!

Doris was laughing again.

It was her, just trying to scare me.

Agnes glared at the both of us, "Shhhh!"

6

"Sorry," I said, but it wasn't really my fault.

"We're not supposed to be here. Come on." She opened the door, shut off the lights, and then locked the door behind us.

We quietly followed her out as she went back to return Key 13, and then back up the elevator to the fifth floor, to the normal part of the hospital. I looked at my watch. It was time for lunch. I wasn't sure if I was that hungry now.

The state hospital has a history going back over 150 years. It had started as a hospital for Civil War wounded, and then became a hospital for the poor. Gradually over time it evolved into basically a warehouse of sorts for people who don't fit into society, or cannot cope with society, or just can't live on their own without assistance. There were the physically disabled, accident victims, the mentally ill, and those who suffered addiction, all people who needed constant care, one way or the other.

As many patients were elderly or in a general weakened condition, occasionally a person would pass away on our watch. Oftentimes, it was a relief to see a person pass on, after seeing them suffer for so long.

The body would have to be prepared to be brought down to the morgue. That meant the body had to be cleaned up, washed, and a clean sheet put over it. We generally did this in teams of two to three people. I had to do this work a few times, I recall. It was no fun, but something we had to do. We would cover the person with a clean sheet, and move the person onto a gurney. We would shut all the doors to all the patients' rooms so they would not see the body being wheeled down the hall, so as to not upset anyone. Then we would pull the gurney along quietly, in a solemn, dignified sort of way, down to the delivery elevator at the end of the dark hallway, so it would not be seen by patients. And that's how it was done, to quietly and respectfully bring the departed on his way down to the morgue—as if it were a waiting room where he would remain until leaving this world and enter into the next. Readers may wonder, did we tie a tag on the person's toe, like you see on TV? No. We did not. We simply cleaned the departed up, and then after covering the person with a sheet, transported him (or her) down to the morgue. Perhaps bodies in big city morgues get a tag on their toe. This was simply a small morgue in a state hospital, nothing special.

Most people who resided at the hospital had family who would claim them and take care of arrangements. Some people, sadly, had no one. No family, no occasional visitors, not ever. The hospital staff, along with fellow patients, was the closest thing some people had to a family.

It was said that there was a paupers' graveyard somewhere on the hospital's grounds, but I never saw it, and to this day do not know of its location. It was also said that the hospital was inhabited by a few ghosts. Unfortunately, I never saw any. Perhaps if I had worked the night shift, I would have seen them drifting about the ward.

After having refuse thrown at me too many times, I began to think about secretarial school and eventually left with only sad memories of the place; memories that continue to haunt me even to this day. I often think back and imagine the tragedy of people existing there, in the state hospital, no visitors, no cards, no letters, with only the television in the day room and their fellow disabled patients for company.

They remain there, waiting until their day comes, the day when staff will ask for Key 13.

(Names have been changed. Story based on actual events. And yes, there really was a two headed baby.)

The Factory

Maxwell, whose real name was MX0001138WL1936, was watching the clock above the assembly line in the factory where he and probably, he guessed, thousands of others like him worked. They were all given a number that was to be their new name for life; and their memories had been erased. But many of them invented names for themselves with the few letters in the numbers they had been given. It was one of the few ways they held onto their humanity, what little humanity there was left in the world, after The Company took over everything.

People weren't supposed to remember, but the erasure process wasn't perfect. Sometimes, just sometimes, people remembered what a blue sky looked like, what clean air smelled like. Other things, like grass, trees, the song of birds . . . and other dangerous ideas that The Company had long ago banned, for the good of society.

He stood next to RL0001066HP1929, also known as Ralph, or Ralphie, as he liked to be called; and he knew Ralph was looking forward to quitting time, too. Soon they would be herded into the transport that carried the vast numbers of working people back to where they existed when not working, and another shift would come and take their place on the assembly line.

They were all constantly reminded to be grateful to The Company for their jobs, and that they could all be very easily replaced by robots. But secretly, Max and Ralph wondered if human life were now so cheap that

The Company used up people rather than purchase robots?

On the viewscreen up above near the digital clock ran a constant stream of commercials praising The Company and all it had done for humanity; but people working through the dullness and repetition had ceased to watch it long ago. The messages scrolling across the screen reminded everyone how lucky they were to have a job working for The Company.

Instead, most of them just watched the clock.

Soon they would go home and watch their viewscreens at home, watch more programming controlled by The Company, and heat up their dull slabs of protein for supper. Ralphie once told Max that he bit down into his protein slab and bit into an actual human finger. "What?"

"Yeah," said Ralph. "I tried to report it, but they said that probably just an air bubble got into the mixture when the machines were mixing all the wonderful vitamins The Company gives us grateful workers and it just looked like a finger. But not to worry, they said they'd replace it with a whole new package. Wasn't that nice of them?!"

"Yeah? Wonder how the hell a finger got in there?"

"Dunno," said Ralph. "Maybe the machinery people work on in the food processing plant isn't so safe after all?" he chuckled. "Wonderful Company that we all work for!" They laughed.

Suddenly the intercom announced that Employee Number MX0001138WL1936 was to report immediately to the office. "What the hell is this about?" Max was worried now. He knew he'd been slow lately, but it was long past the time when people used to be allowed to retire. People weren't allowed to retire anymore. The Company didn't give out pensions. No one knew why, but The Company probably made it that way for everyone's own good.

When Max arrived at the office he was greeted by the Supervisory Robot that everyone on the factory floor reported to. It was a standard model Supervisory Robot with a dull matte gray finish and chrome trim.

"Congratulations, Employee Number MX0001138WL1936," it said in its gentle electronic voice, "You have been chosen to be transferred to the Food Processing Plant. Your labors at the new work location will be much more enjoyable! On behalf of The Most Glorious Company, we are thankful for your service in this factory! The transport to the new work location awaits you, Employee Number MX0001138WL1936. Please hurry along—"

"Oh screw your damn circuit board," Max mumbled.

"I assure you, Employee Number MX0001138WL1936, my circuit board is screwed in tightly and functioning properly."

"Never mind." He hated these robots, but they ran everything now. Humans had long ago disappeared from supervisory and administrative positions. No one knew why. Another Company decision for the benefit of society.

"Please gather your belongings and hurry to meet your transport, Employee Number MX0001138WL1936."

Max hurried to his locker to get what little he had. He would miss Ralphie. He would miss having someone to joke around with. Ralphie hated the supervisory robots as much as he did, maybe even worse.

Finally, he went out back toward the delivery entrance and go on the transport. As soon as he boarded, he realized it wasn't a vehicle for transporting people at all. He had been put into an equipment truck. No seats, no windows, no . . . nothing. What the hell kind of ride to his new job was this? Finally the vehicle stopped moving and the door opened into darkness. He looked around and finally his eyes adjusted as there was only minimal light, and what he saw shocked him.

He was dropped off into what appeared to be a warehouse filled with people, many of them sitting on the concrete floor, some standing around looking forlorn, and some leaning against the concrete walls.

"What the hell is this place?" he asked out loud, hoping someone, anyone, would dare to answer.

"This is the food processing plant, what else?" said one man sitting off in the corner by himself, not looking up, just staring at the floor he sat on.

"Max!"

Suddenly, he heard a soft voice.

"Max! Is that you? It's me! Tish!"

He recognized her coming toward him; it was Tish, otherwise known as TSH1149CV159188, "Max! Oh no. They sent you here, too?"

They worked together for years, until one day very recently she didn't report to work. The others on work crew were told by the robots that ran the factory that she had just been promoted, and that they should all be proud of her. "Well, she could have said goodbye," he thought, but now he wondered what it was really all about.

She came closer and put her arms around him briefly, then suddenly took a step back, a look of sadness on her face.

"Hey, Tish! What the hell is going on? The stupid machine that owns all our jobs tells me I'm being transferred to an easier job at the food factory, and now I end up here? What the hell is this place? Why is everybody just waiting around? I don't understand any of this."

"Max! This is the food processing plant. Max . . . I don't know how to tell you this, so I'll just say it. It's terrible. We're all waiting to be processed."

A week later Ralphie sat alone at the table in the company break room, about to sadly bite into his protein slab. He truly hated the protein slabs the workers were given out, day after day, the same dull pink protein slabs, no change in flavor, but full of wonderful vitamins and nutrition and so good for you, they were all told.

He'd flush it down the toilet if he wasn't so hungry.

He missed Max. He hoped Max was happy wherever he was now, and wished Max was sitting opposite him on the other side of the table where he always used to be. They always had lunch together and joked around, making fun of the Supervisory Robot and anything else they could complain about on the job.

Finally Ralph took a bite out of the slab and out of loneliness he imagined Max was with him now and imagined they were having lunch together like always . . .

Into The Crusher

November 12, 2072

Arrived after midnight, so I made pretty good time. Unpacked the car—Beatrice's old Mercedes. She gave it to me after getting a new one, and it's good that she did so as the car has plenty of room to carry miscellaneous items; and because it's over ten years old, it fits in well with the other cars in the area—although most of them are seriously dented and rusting. This one is in good shape, she kept her up well—her engine is strong, and there's hardly a scratch in her silken ebony finish.

It is the beginning of the holiday season, and soon people will want to begin their shopping; yet this city is so decayed, so impoverished, I do not know how the people will manage. Perhaps if we are successful here with this endeavor the following years will be better for everyone, ourselves included.

Parked the Mercedes in an alley. Hope she'll be safe, for many of the creatures lurking about this part of the city look as if they would steal away with anything not nailed down to the damned pavement.

November 13, 2072

Woke up at dusk. Fortunately, the windows face east for more darkness when the sun finally leaves the sky. Looked down into the alley to check on Blackie. Still there in one piece, no fenders or wheels missing, and so I felt incredibly lucky.

Pulled my first meal in this desolate place from the small portable refrigerator, opened the bottle, and heated it in the micro. Drank it slowly while gazing into the city's blackness and felt a deep cold loneliness from within. The night is not the same without the rest of my people around me. I hope for a good future, and look to the time when many of them will join me here.

For now, Beatrice's car is the only familiar thing I have with me. I miss Beatrice, and think of her often...

November 14, 2072

On this night I finally began wandering about the ancient factory complex that I was "volunteered" to check out. It's just nothing but dark corridors, empty spaces, dust, rats, roaches, a few unused and vandalized dust covered machines, and, of course, a great vast amount of shattered windows surround the place, letting the wind blast howling through constantly, creating a miserably cold draft. Well, what else did I expect?

And! On the lower level there seems to be a colony of assorted homeless persons. I approached slowly in the dark, very quietly, and watched. Did not attempt contact. It would be most dangerous to do so now. Since the larger world "accidentally" discovered us some time ago, there is still a great distrust—bigotry is what I call it. Perhaps it will always be so. The new awareness that we are not just myth doesn't make our long lives easier. But . . . I watched the people. Most seemed not to be junkies; many had women and children with them: entire families, circled around a fire lit up in an old rusted metal trashcan, trying to stay warm. Entire families. One small group of people even had a dog, a skinny little mutt, shivering in the cold at his master's feet.

I almost wanted to rush out to greet them, the ones capable of working, to tell them we plan to open up a new processing facility here soon. But no. Must go slowly. They won't want to trust us. They would likely imagine we are all here moving in just to feed on their misery.

November 15, 2072

Woke to discover the rest of my things had been delivered to the entrance of this horrible place. Carried everything up alone. Even for me, much of it was heavy. Later, I remained in due to the storm, watched the battery powered television. Another bombing. More stupid terrorism. A jet blown away in mid-air. When will they ever learn? Will they never cease to be violent animals? I should not think this way. I need to work with these people, after all.

At times, though, I only want to run from them. And far.

November 16, 2072

Woke up as usual, looked out the window and got totally bored. Of course I was—there is nothing to do here. Not in this town. A half century ago it was a busy city, alive. With the economy the way it has been the past few decades, it is all just dead, or nearly so. Many businesses are closed down, storefronts boarded up, except for a few. Homes look empty and abandoned. The city is a vast ocean of empty buildings, bombed or burnt out from last year's riots, all darkened, not an electric light is in use, save for a few, dotting brightly like lone stars outside my small frost covered window. . . .

It is much worse here than we thought.

I wandered out to search for a newspaper, or magazine, not being interested in the television. On my return I found a homeless man sleeping in the hallway, a bottle emptied beside him, and quite out of it. Threw my coat over him; the cold could kill him sooner than it would me. And then I stalked off, left him in his own world.

Read the dull paper all through, read the "latest news and updates" on the massacre as well—only a small paragraph about the "slow investigation, due to the lack of hard evidence." Ten of us were butchered in our sleep. What the hell evidence do these idiots need?

The authorities are really just happy to be rid of a few of us, most likely. That's why we've got to move, start over, and hope this won't happen again.

November 17, 2072

Mort, as he simply likes to be called—and he will not give his last name, says he has none, was wandering about the upper level, and so I ran into him as I went out of my hiding place to explore the rat infested building a little more. He did not see me, at first, but I followed him through the dark and finally let him see me in the weak moonlight that glowed through the dust filled cracked windows. He said he knew someone was up here, he had seen a different car in the neighborhood, had seen things being delivered, and etc. And he was curious. I took the coat back, although it smells like him now.

I let him come up to my small space to clean up in the primitive shower that was set in place before I arrived—along with the tiny fridge and uncomfortable furniture. Fortunately we found some plumbing still functional when we bought the building, dirt cheap, last year.

Mort was amazed to see such "comfort"—my battery powered TV, refrigerator, unsoiled clothing, and a place to wash. He assumed at first I must be as lost as he is, like all the others down below. But I explained that I am exploring the place. He does not understand, so I decide, wisely I think, to not get into it. Not yet.

Perhaps he imagines I am a criminal, a drug dealer on the run? I might as well be. We all must live in hiding, especially in this century.

November 18, 2072

Beatrice arrived with a delivery packed in ice, in the trunk of her new sports car. And not a moment too soon, for I was nearly out of it.

We walked around the factory, just to see the dust and debris, then worked our way around the city. It was totally dark. I remember not too long ago when cities were bright with the harsh glare of electricity. Now the town can't even afford that. Everything is shut down when not in use.

November 19, 2072

We returned close to dawn last night, slept through the day. It was wonderful to just have her in the same room, breathe the same air, and sleep under the same roof. She had to leave tonight. There is still much to be done back home, before the move.

Wandered around some more after she left. Found Mort had been trying to follow me. What the hell. Of course my sudden appearance on the top level, complete with furniture and television, seems odd. So I'll let him hang around. Got to start somewhere. I let him up to watch TV.

He seems harmless enough. After all, we're both outcasts in this society—if we can pretend that there is any sort of society left in this world.

If only he would wash more.

November 20, 2072

Well it was due to happen sooner or later—I hoped for later. But no. It was sooner.

He was watching television, more news on the latest riots and shootings, and suddenly he wanted to go for food. He had turned in enough cans and bottles to buy cheap fast food, so he said. But I got up to get it for him; didn't take his money. He needs it more than I do. I've got plenty for now. And, actually, I just wanted to get some fresh air.

So I went. The fast food place was too brightly lit, and smelled bad, very bad. But I returned, happy to be out of there.

He had gone into the refrigerator, said he was looking for a beer.

So . . . I handed Mort the warm fast food package, and said, "Well, here's yours, I'll just get mine," and went for the fridge myself.

In the old days when we had to hide, and we still do, it wasn't labeled and dated for freshness the way it is now. So Mort must've read the label and freaked out when he did. He must've freaked out big time. But I stayed cool.

He looked at me and held onto the bag loosely, almost dropping it, stared at me coldly, "Y-you . . . you're a . . . you're a—"

"Yeah. Right. Look, it's not really such a big deal, okay?" and I slipped it into the micro, "I mean, we're no secret anymore, right?" He had this awful look on his face, like he would bolt for the door, "Come on, Mort, we're both outcasts."

He still didn't like it, so I tried, "Hey, wanna job?" It broke the spell.

I spent the rest of the night telling all, where I came from, what I'm really all about, about the deal we've already got with the slaughterhouses, the factory building bought and paid for, the bottling machinery to come. All we needed were the people. And we are too few. "So, I figured I could hang out a month ahead of time, get to know the neighborhood, find some out of work people, looks like there's plenty of them, and, well . . . that's it, Mort. Plain and simple. The facility will eventually ship livestock blood all over the northeast. We'll need drivers for the refrigerated trucks, some office personnel, people to load the trucks; at least 300 new jobs, maybe more if it all works out," and he was silent while I spoke, disturbingly quiet.

"Shit!" he finally said, almost with a laugh, "I seen one a you guys on TV, when I still had a roof."

"No, Mort, don't pay any attention to those stupid movies, okay?"

"Not, like, it was a late night talk show, that what's his name."

Roderick Moroy was whom he meant. The activist. He was always on TV. "Oh yeah, him," and I had met him once, very outspoken. "Yeah, I know, he does the media thing, just trying to make people think, I guess," and his wife was often on television too. I was stunned to see him marry a non-vampire but many of us do, there's so few of us around. I often wondered if she liked the publicity. And figured she probably did.

"Hey, I thought it was all a hoax, man."

"No, it's not. It's real. It's been real for thousands of years. Only in the twentieth century did people not believe, and now they believe again. Well. Here we are. Hello," and he looked at me strangely.

"Sorry," I said, "poor attempt at humor." But he seemed to be thinking deeply.

It was nearly dawn, I let him sleep on a blanket on my floor, gave him my pillow.

"Well," he said, "your fridge is full, so I guess you won't eat me."

"Hell no." Certainly not. I wondered if he had fleas.

November 23, 2072

Been busy these past few nights. Mort has been showing me around the 'hood, letting me know where the junkies hang out and where to stay away from, and where the generally down on their luck types camp out. The people naturally assume I'm new on the streets or something. He is a tremendous help. He even showed me the entranceways the homeless used to get into the factory for shelter from the cold. When they all have homes, we shall board them up.

And Mort seems quite interested in me, and asks all sorts of questions about our kind. I do not mind, although a few of them are awfully ridiculous. For instance, he is certain we have got this mysterious power over women, or something. Hell, if a hooker tries to do business with me on the streets, she just wants a fast buck. But no. He is sure I can draw them to me. I can only think about Beatrice at times like this.

November 24, 2072

Soon it will be one of their holidays, and many have nowhere to go. I feel bad for them all when only I am fed well. I almost wish that I could share what I have, but they would find it repulsive.

Beatrice came again, to deliver more, and spend some time. I introduced Mort, who has become an attachment lately. Really, he can wear one down. And I struggled to find a polite way to get him out of my place for a few hours. What relief. . . .

Beatrice. . . .

Finally in my arms after so long, so painfully long.

I did not want her to leave, but she had to go before the end of the night. And I do not want her in this city, not until we all find a safer place to lock ourselves in for the day.

I shall work on that next.

Maybe Mort will help. Or maybe not. Perhaps he almost seems somehow too enthusiastic about helping me. I wonder about that.

November 25, 2072

Mort is back in my life again tonight. I write this as he sleeps in front of the television, the opiate of the masses. He is a good fellow, but very determined to study me: he wants to know how strong, how old, how tough, etc. I try not to bore the guy.

The night is quiet. Too quiet. Perhaps most are huddled in corners, in abandoned buildings like this one, on air grates, in cardboard boxes, while the upper classes eat well and stay warm. It all just sickens me.

November 26, 2072

I should have seen this coming. Mort finally asked it. Make me like you. Oh shit.

"I wanna be immortal," he says. I've never heard that one before, but a lot of us get hit with this sort of thing. People are such jerks about that. Here we go again.

"I cannot do this. That's only a myth. We're born this way," case closed, I thought. Oh no. Not quite. He thinks I'm holding out on him.

"But I was so good to you, man," and etc. I should have known. He played me for a fool.

November 27, 2072

Have not seen Mort this evening. Perhaps I am lucky, but somehow I worry still. He was extremely angry that I would not, could not, grant his wish. Drove the Mercedes around a bit, just for fun, with the windows opened, so the frigid air would clear my head. Again I am alone, without my own kind, or any kind. I decided to just start the car and wander aimlessly through the eternal blackness of this forsaken city.

Returned before dawn, the car's tank nearly emptied, and my own soul feeling empty. I went in, ascended the back stairs to my so-called home, and drank my fill gazing at the murky gray dawn.

November 28, 2072

Saw Mort again, and now I should really be worried. Down below my window, talking to a crowd of people. Yes. Now I am very concerned. I shall begin moving everything I can carry to another end of the building.

November 29, 2072

Finished relocating, and the place is dead quiet. I was probably being foolish to worry about it. We spend all our long lives worrying about Them.

Took a walk, as usual. But, strangely, the camp of homeless people had moved away. Perhaps they found a warmer place. I hope so. The winters are so bitter here.

November 30, 2072

I should have known. It's over. And I blew it. The deal is off, because of my mistake.

Again I saw Mort, and again he was talking to a crowd. He was loud, so I could hear him. "They're coming! Hundreds of them. It's an invasion! In another month, this city will fill up with vampires, and there will be no place to hide!"

I ducked swiftly down into an alley as he shouted; being able to see well in the dark has its advantages. What should I do? I am lost in this barren concrete and steel wilderness, surrounded by enemies.

December 1, 2072

Beatrice managed to find my new hiding place. She is here, now, by my side in this storage room. We have barricaded ourselves against the people. The only light is an almost used up candle. We need nothing else, save for each other.

They are still out there. We hear voices, footsteps.

When they finally go away, we will try and run for the car, if it is still out there.

Right now, I hear him out there grumbling. It's Mort.

"I know they're in there, damn them, I saw them go up this way."

Beatrice is silent. She is backed up against the corner. If we speak, if we move, they will hear us. If only we could arm ourselves, but we have nothing.

It is several hours, I believe, since the last entry. It is quiet now. Beatrice is slowly beginning to remove the crates and boxes we placed up against the heavy steel door. She whispers to me, they seem to have left. We shall head directly to the car, immediately get out of this wretched hellhole of a city, and never return.

The above paragraphs are selected excerpts from a small leather bound journal discovered by auto wrecking yard personnel under the seat of a fire-damaged vehicle shortly before it was crushed for recycling. The vehicle's owner(s) could not be located. Police have decided not to investigate the matter any further, citing "lack of enough strong evidence of any wrong doing or foul play."

Family Secrets

We weren't ever supposed to talk about it, not ever. That's why it's been so many years; I almost feel like I could forget it even happened. Well, no, not really. Something like that, you never forget. But I look out where the pigpen used to be, and it's like it was so long ago, it almost doesn't matter anymore.

It was well over fifty years ago, maybe. We were just kids, then. Back then, things were different. Way different. You didn't talk about some things then, the way they talk about things today. When things happened, nobody talked. Nobody. Things were kept quiet. It was as if there was more shame in talking about something, than there was in actually doing the horrible thing that you were talking about.

I guess it's okay to talk now. Mama has been dead for years, and we were just kids. So probably no one will care. It all happened about a year after Mama let Uncle Roger stay with us. We weren't sure about Uncle Roger, well, because there was just something about him we weren't sure about. But Mama said he was family, and families look out for each other. Uncle Roger had been in some kind of trouble, she said, but she would never say what kind of trouble he had been in. We always wondered about that, but being kids, we didn't dare ask.

We weren't supposed to tell our friends that Uncle Roger was staying with us. We didn't know why that was, either. But again, we were just kids, so we did what we were told, and didn't ask questions that we weren't supposed to ask. Kids did what they were told then, mostly.

But then I saw something happen to my brother Marvin behind the barn. Uncle Roger turned and saw me standing there, so he took off back to the house. Marvin was about eight, I believe. I was fourteen. I asked Marvin after Uncle Roger disappeared into the house and Marvin said that Uncle Roger had been doing things like that since he had arrived, and that he had been told to keep quiet, and that Mama wouldn't believe him if he told her. I told Marvin that it was weird and that I didn't like it, but I was just a kid, too, and I really didn't know what it was all about. Kids didn't know much back then. I mean we knew some things about girls and boys but we didn't know about strange things like that. No one ever told us about things like that. Things like that, I know now that things happened, but since people didn't talk, it was pretty much unheard of back then.

It's a small town now. It was an even smaller town then. We were out in the country, and any authorities you could go to were far away. We didn't even have a phone back then. We just had the farm, the animals, and the old car that usually ran okay. Our father had been dead for years, and Mama was glad for Uncle Roger to come and maybe help out. Working a farm is a lot for one woman and two kids. We needed an extra hand. But Uncle Roger didn't help much. He mostly just drank and hung around. It quickly dawned on me that he wasn't much use.

I came into the house and Marvin followed me, telling me not to say anything. And I wasn't going to say anything. I was really going to try to keep quiet. But when I got into the house and saw Uncle Roger sitting at the table with his whisky and Mama trying to get dinner ready after working all day around the farm herself, I guess I kind of lost it. I still to this day do not know if I did the right thing. But I guess I kind of lost it when I saw Uncle Roger sitting there, doing nothing much but downing his whisky and pouring himself another one. So I did what most people back then would never do.

I told.

That's when Mama just flipped a switch, I guess. For all her life she was a quiet woman who just did her work and didn't say much. She always just got up before dawn and had us do our chores before getting us off to school, and on Sunday she got us off to church. I never heard her raise her voice, or ever saw her raise her hand.

But I told.

Mama had been making a pie, and she had her big heavy wooden rolling pin in her hand when I told. She just looked up, opened her eyes, looked at me, and then looked at Uncle Roger.

Uncle Roger didn't have a chance to say anything. He was down on the floor with one blow. She was a strong woman. She wasn't a big woman, but she was strong from constantly doing the heavy work. She was a widow and had to do a lot of the work herself. I heard a crack when the rolling pin landed on his head. It must have cracked his skull. He was flat on the floor and didn't move, and so we all thought he was dead right then and there.

"Damn it," she said, and she almost never swore, "I knew he was no damn good. If he wasn't family, I'd never have taken him in. I guess those folks who were out looking for him when he came here had a reason to. Now he's gone and made the same kind of trouble here."

"What are we gonna do?" I said.

"Boys," she said, "Take him outside. I'll have to mop this floor."

Mama always took pride in her clean kitchen, and now there was blood all over the floor.

Me and Marvin, we dragged him out into the backyard. He was heavy, but we managed. Marvin said that he was surprised Mama believed him, because Uncle Roger always said that Mama would never believe. I said, "Well, Mama knows Uncle Roger better than we do, I guess."

It was late fall and already getting dark out, and we would have to figure out something soon. We dragged him out into the backyard, and he started to whimper and moan.

"Boys!" Mama called out from the back door, "Go get the shovel out of the tool shed."

"He's alive, Mama," said Marvin. "He's alive, and I'm scared."

"Don't be scared," I said, "He ain't gonna hurt yah no more."

"Well, boys, you gotta finish the job. Don't I always tell yah that yah gotta always finish things?"

"Yes, Mama," Marvin said, "But what are we gonna do?"

Uncle Roger was flat on the cold ground, and he was moaning and mumbling. Suddenly his eyes opened up wide, "Gonna kill you!" But he didn't get up. He just lay there like an old empty sack of nothing.

"Boys, supper is almost ready. You gotta do something quick. I don't want dinner to be ruined. Just toss Uncle Roger into the pigpen. Those pigs will eat anything."

31

"Okay, Mama," I said.

And that's what we did. We dragged him over to the pigpen and gave him to the pigs, and then we went back into the house and heard Uncle Roger yell out this awful scream. We just went in and sat at the table. Mama had made chicken pot pie, and a nice blueberry pie too. We ate and didn't talk much. We could still hear him screaming out there. By the time we were ready to eat the blueberry pie the screaming stopped. Mama did the dishes and we did our homework and went to bed.

The next morning I got up to milk the cows and there was nothing left in the pigpen. Mama sent us off to school and said not to worry, and that no one will miss him much. If a deputy came around, we weren't supposed to say much, except that Uncle Roger had stayed awhile and then left. We just didn't know where he had gone off to. And that was that.

No one ever came around looking for Uncle Roger. We grew up like normal boys and didn't talk ever about it. Marvin didn't do so well, though. When I got back from Vietnam he had gotten into drugs. He overdosed one day. It was the end of him. Some say it was suicide. Maybe it was. Maybe the nightmares he always had drove him to it. Then Mama found out she had cancer and it wasn't long for her. I got married and had a few kids. I hoped they would stay and keep the farm but they went away to the city. My wife and I hired some people to help out around here. Not many of them stayed very long. I don't know why. Maybe they just don't like the hard work. I don't raise pigs anymore. I've had everything else. Cows, sheep, chickens, turkeys, and goats. No more pigs. I haven't raised pigs in a long time. My kids grew up, I never told them. I never told my wife. She died of a heart attack one day. It was sudden. I'm not sure if I should have told her before she died, so she would know why I wouldn't let her plant her flower garden over there.

I never told anyone.

The doctor says I have cancer now. It won't be long for me. Maybe it runs in the family. Maybe I have to tell someone before I die. That's another thing that runs in the family. We all kept quiet about it, all these years.

Sometimes I sit on the back porch and look over to the patch of grass where the pigpen was and just look at it. When she was alive, my wife would ask why I always look over there, like I was looking at nothing. I like to think I forgot about it, but I can't, really. And sometimes, on a cold night, when I sit in the house alone, I can hear a man scream. Then it goes away. Or I think it goes away, like a distant memory. But it never really does. It's awful to be in the house alone, on a cold night, and hear that scream. I don't hear it every night. Just in the fall, around dusk, or on a cold dark night, like the night it happened. Maybe it's my imagination playing tricks on me. Maybe I'm just getting old. Or maybe there's still something out there, something left in that ground where it happened.

Something evil.

Things like that, you can never really forget, no matter how hard you try.

Night Comes to the City

Kirstie gazed around at the rest of the crowd waiting for the city bus, and then she realized that she was the only one to notice it, though she had never realized it before—it was that no one on the street corner looked at each other, spoke to each other, or even noticed the person next to them. They were all locked into their own world, oblivious to the world around them. Oblivious. That was the right word. And she had been too. Only today, it suddenly dawned on her that she had been riding the same bus for years with the same people and never spoke to them, noticed them, or knew their names. Like her, they worked at their dull repetitive little jobs, collected their low pay, and went home to their TV sets and tasteless microwave dinners. That was the world that everyone lived in. It was deadly boring, but there was nothing anyone could do about it. *Nothing!*

The bus pulled up to the corner, she rose up from the bench she sat on, and got in line. As usual, she sat by the window, looked out at the buildings, watched the homeless people push their carts as they made their way down the streets, and she looked down into the dark alleyways cluttered with typical city garbage.

Something moved down there. She tried to look again, but it was gone.

It was only a brief moment as the bus went by, but she saw it: As large as a dog, yet not a dog. It was gray, with a leathery tail, short fur, red eyes, a pointed snout, and small rounded ears. She almost laughed, but remained quiet. If she didn't know better, she would have thought it was a giant rat. But that wasn't possible. There was no such thing.

A giant rat. Yeah, right. Her life was getting to her. The bus arrived at her stop.

As usual dinner consisted of something tasteless. At least the nightly news was interesting. Brenda, her roommate, finally stopped yapping about being stood up again by her useless boyfriend Dirk. Kirstie went to the fridge and got a beer and they sat and vegetated in front of the TV. Police apprehended a self-declared animal liberation activist after he allegedly released a number of laboratory animals from a research facility. The video switched to the clip of the suspect being hauled away by police. A large overweight man with long gray hair shouted madly, "Free! Free! They all have a right to be free! All life has its purpose on Mother Earth! They all have a right to be free! FREE!" The camera followed him as he was dragged, kicking and screaming, to the squad car.

The bland face of the announcer returned on screen. "A spokesperson for the research facility denies allegations that any of the animals released may have been dangerous. In other local news today, a family searches for their missing cat."

The television showed a middle-aged woman crying wildly as her family stood soberly by her side. "I just hope deep in my broken sad heart and I pray to God Almighty that He will send His angels to speak to whoever has my dear precious and beloved Fluffy so they will send her back to her loving home!"

"Now, why is that news?"

"Hey!" Brenda suddenly sat up and looked alert. "Isn't that the lady who lives downstairs on the first floor, right below this dump?"

"Yeah, and she takes the bus every day and sits behind me too. I never knew her name until tonight." The television revealed her name to be Mrs. Kleagle.

"Cool. Our crappy neighborhood is on TV!"

"I'll tell yah what's even more cool, Bren," Kirstie remembered what she saw lurking down the alley, "I think there's a giant rat loose in this neighborhood."

"What? You're nuts."

"Nope! I am like totally serious," Kirstie explained everything in detail, "and yah know what? I think it escaped from that lab!"

"What if it ate that lady's cat?"

"What if it eats some little kid?"

"What if it might eat us?"

"What if that nut let lose thousands of them?"

"Oh my God, like now I am so scared!"

They sat alone together in the darkness, their only light the glare of the TV. Night had come to the city. Chaos had now entered into their monotonous lives. From deep down in the alley below their window rose a high-pitched shriek followed by a low wail.

Brenda giggled. Kirstie got up and looked out the window, "Cool!"

The loud blast of the clock radio woke her up, not with the usual rock music, but this time with reports of local sightings of an alleged giant rat.

Residents have reported seeing a strange rodent-like creature the size of a large dog roaming city streets and frightening family pets . . . Police call these claims ridiculous and have declined to investigate the issue further . . . The stock market rebounded today as Wall Street once again breathed a sigh of relief, the Dow Jones closing at . . .

A half of an hour later, Kirstie went to look out the window and down into the alley again. Her curling iron was hanging out of her dark blonde hair. Half of her makeup was on. She wore the oversized T-shirt she had slept in. She was trying to get ready for the job she hated and investigate the rat at the same time, "Look at this. The trashcans are spilled out all over the alley. There is garbage everywhere."

"It was the rat!" They both knew that they should have felt terrified, but instead they laughed uncontrollably. There was nothing else they could do about it.

Kirstie looked behind where she sat on the bus. There she was. It was Mrs. Kleagle, looking composed and unexcited now that the news camera wasn't nearby. "Oh, Mrs. Kleagle, I am so sorry to hear about your cat!"

The middle-aged woman suddenly snapped back into alertness, "Oh. Thank you, dear. You're the nice girl who lives upstairs from us. I can't remember your name?" Mrs. Kleagle had never really met her. She had merely lived in the same building and had ridden the same bus for several years, but the two never spoke to each other.

"Kirstie. Kirstie Fletcher. Yeah. I hope you find your little kitty."

Suddenly, for the first time ever, the bus came alive with conversation.

The dark haired man with the Spanish accent declared that his wife's poodle was also missing, "And I am glad that smelly thing is gone!"

"Yeah?" said the man who looked like an aging hippie, "A lot of strange things happening around here lately. Missing animals. Missing kids. Missing socks. It could be a conspiracy. I blame the government myself."

"Did anyone else hear that awful scream last night?" said the blonde woman with the short skirt and bad dye job, "It was like so bizarre."

"The radio says there's a giant rat!" yelped the kid with purple hair. He always wore the same leather clothes every day and carried his electric guitar.

"I think I saw it," Kirstie whispered cautiously.

"It got loose from a lab!" said the man who dressed like a stockbroker, "It's those darned liberals. They set loose all the animals. They all got big on the radiation experiments. And now they're loose on this society!" He spoke loudly, then he immediately went back to reading the financial section of his paper.

"I still say it's the damn government," said the old hippie. "It's a conspiracy."

"Oh no, my poor precious Fluffy!" Mrs. Kleagle reached into her purse for a handkerchief and sobbed wildly. People went to sit by her side and comfort her. Kirstie reached out to hold her hand.

The bus driver looked up and watched the action from the rearview mirror, "Hey, then again, you know, it could be the aliens."

The data entry and paperwork she processed was dull as usual, but on this day people in the office had

38

something outside of their cheating boyfriends and trouble with their screwed up families to talk about. At lunch she walked to the corner store to get a sandwich and while she stood in line people at the counter joked about a monster rat high on steroids being on the loose. When she left the sandwich shop a group of teenagers hanging out on the street corner called out, "Hey, lady. Look out for the big rat!" She looked in their direction and laughed. They laughed along with her. Back at work the supervisor who almost never spoke except to criticize drifted by her desk, "So, what do you think about this giant rat nonsense?" Kirstie did not want to admit that she had seen the monster, so she pretended to be absolutely fascinated by her work, which she wasn't.

Back on the bus, the conversation continued and became more involved. This time the young mother who rode the bus each afternoon with her three spoiled runny-nose brats expressed her concern to the graying hippie that she previously had never spoken to or even looked at. He listened, and he appeared to be tremendously interested in everything she had to say, "I really feel that this thing that is loose out there is a threat to my children. I mean, I am really very concerned. In fact, I am outraged that something like this would be permitted to escape from their facility. This is a real threat to our society and our society's children. People who are this irresponsible have no concern for our children's well-being, and—"

"Mommy! I gotta go to the—"

"You just shut the hell up when Mommy is talking damn it!"

Kirstie looked around and noticed that the lady with the bright blonde hair who always wore a mini-skirt was showing Mrs. Kleagle photos of her Persian cat, her Chihuahua, her ferret, and her blue macaw, "and this is my little Killer eating out of her favorite dish!"

The kid with the purple hair sat behind them and looked over the photos as well, "I always wanted a python myself. When I get my recording deal, I'm getting a snake."

The Spanish man, the stockbroker, and the hippie now sat up front together with the bus driver speaking quietly, "Okay, so you say it's a government conspiracy, and you say it's because of the damned liberals, and you say it's because the CIA is letting drugs flow into the lower income neighborhoods. But maybe you're all looking at the wrong things. Because They all want us to look at all the wrong things. If we all look at the wrong things, then we'll all be fighting amongst ourselves when They land and take over! Don't yah get it? It's the aliens! They're behind the giant rat, and big foot, inflation, and the hole in the ozone layer. They caused the oil crisis in '73. We, the human race, have got to wake up in time to resist!"

The bus came to a halt, the door swung open. People exited quietly, but their minds were all very disturbed.

When she came home to the small, cramped, dimly lit and messy apartment, Brenda was arguing over the phone with Dirk. "What? You're making fun of me? Are you laughing at me, Dirk? Because it's true. I heard it howling down in the alley outside our place. Kirstie saw it running through the street the other day. It's as big as a

40

for God's sake dinosaur! I am like totally serious! Dirk? Dirk! That's it, Dirk. If you keep on making fun of me, we are through!" She slammed down the phone and turned to look at Kirstie, "We are through! I'd rather date a rat!" They laughed together.

"Maybe your boyfriend is the rat we're all looking for!"

"Yeah, right."

That night dinner consisted of the pizza and beer Brenda had intended to bring to Dirk's place. They watched the video that was also intended for Dirk. *The Beast From Beyond Time and Space!* It was black and white and made in 1956, and it truly stank. The girls were bored until they heard the terrifying shriek that came once more from below their windows.

"Oh my God. Oh my God! I am so scared. I am gonna call Dirk!"

"No! Don't you dare go back to that useless idiot! We'll deal with it ourselves."

"How? Kirstie? What are you gonna do?"

Kirstie got up from the cheap, worn out, second hand couch with a large cold slice of pizza in her hand, "I want to see this monster up close and personal."

"No! Don't! You'll get killed!"

But she did not hesitate. She went out the door, down the stairs and towards the exit that led into the dark alley. With the dim glow of the streetlight she saw it. It was as gray as a wolf, with red eyes, a tail like pale leather, naked paws ending in sharp talons that resembled those on a wild bird of prey. It looked up at her, sniffed the air, and made a chattering sound.

Kirstie tossed the slice of pizza.

41

It grabbed it up in its front paws, sat up on its hind legs, and began to nibble the pizza. Kirstie almost laughed and asked it if it wanted a cold beer to go with that, but she felt foolish and remained silent. The rat finished the pizza and squeaked quietly. Its whiskers twitched, and its pink nose had a piece of cheese stuck to it.

Now at the same height, they looked at each other, eye to eye.

"Don't ever let them catch you! That man was right. You should be free." She turned and went back inside.

Brenda had watched everything from the window above.

"Brenda, that monster has done more for all the people in this neighborhood than all the stupid social programs that the useless government can think up."

"Huh?"

"As long as that rat stays running free, people talk to each other. The have something to be interested in. They get to know each other, they start to look out for each other and each other's kids. They have an escape from their boredom. Because of that mutant rat, we all now have a reason to live, whereas before we all just went to work and came home to stare at four walls."

"What the hell are you talking about?"

"Don't you get it? People need monsters! We all do."

"Huh?"

"They come into our lives to stir things up, they frighten us and force us to relate to each other. They make us wonder about the universe, so they make us actually begin to think. We need monsters, no matter what kind of monsters they are. We need aliens, big foot,

42

UFO's, whatever crap you want to believe in. We need government conspiracies, we need to worry about lab experiments gone wrong, *and we need giant rats to run loose in this city.* The man was right. All things have a purpose here on earth.

"That's the meaning of it all. The monster rat got free from the lab where it was caged up, and when it did, it set us all free along with it. Free from the meaningless routine of our useless lives."

The phone rang, making them both suddenly jump.

Brenda picked it up, *"Hello? Oh. It's you. I told you it's over! Now get lost!"*

Evil Joe

I know it's strange to just say it like this, but Joe was evil. I don't mean that he was messed up, or disturbed, or anything like that. He was evil. Really. Joe was evil. It's true. I know what evil looks like. Let me tell you this. Evil is good looking, and evil talks real cool. Evil has a lot of money, and evil drives a Cadillac.

Nowadays people just don't use that word. Evil. They say someone isn't coping well, something like that. But I really do know that Joe was in fact evil.

Someone your age thinks that it all happened a long time ago. But the seventies weren't that long ago. And I was a lot like you then. I was pretty and young, and from a small town. Yeah. I know. I don't look like much now. But I looked good then. Got a cigarette in that bag? Give me one. I need to quit. My lungs are shot all the way to hell, like the rest of me. But I can't tell this without having a smoke. I came here looking for work too. I was nineteen, and had nothing. He was 37 and he had a lot.

My father took off when I was a kid; we never knew where he went. I decided to come here for work, start out as a cocktail waitress, and learn my way around. My mother and some of my friends were against my coming here. They said no good things could happen, all kinds of people around here. You see, I was also looking to find someone rich, someone who would take care of me, fairy tale stuff like that. Now I know how stupid I was. But it was a small town, no one went to college.

I saw Joe when he was playing poker. I was serving drinks. He was winning big. That's what attracted me to him. He was the winner. He looked rich too. He wore lots of gold, a silk shirt, and had an attitude to go with it. Everyone thought he was cool, all us girls did. There was an older lady who worked there, she was the head waitress. She told us to stay the hell away from him. I wish I'd listened. The other girls did.

He wanted me, and let me know it. He asked me when I get off work. I went home with him that night. He rode me to his place in his Cadillac. It was my first time. He pretty much forced himself onto me. I guess I can't call it a rape, because I didn't say no, and I wanted to be with him. But he was so rough. I should have left him then. I should have gone back to work and forgot all about him. Maybe I should have just gone home. But I didn't.

I moved in with him. He had a nice place; and he paid for everything. At first, things were okay between us. I wasn't happy with the relationship, but I wanted to be with someone like Joe. Any rich ass could have taken his place. It wasn't about love, or sex, or even about the money he spent on me. I guess it was about me being with the most arrogant bastard in town. It made me cool, because he was cool. I guess that's cool by association. I didn't love him, and he didn't love me. Our love life sucked, or I felt like it did. He paid for everything, but I still kept my job because I liked bragging to the other girls about being with Joe. Joe's big car, Joe's big money, Joe's big gun collection. "What does he do for a living? Where does he get all his money?" they would ask. I really should have thought about that.

I came from nothing. I still had nothing when I was with Joe. Maybe even less, because when I was with Joe, I didn't really have myself. But Joe made me feel like I was something, because I was seen with him, I went home with him, rode in his car, wore the slutty clothes he picked out for me. He pushed people around at the club, he beat people up in the parking lot, and scared the shit out of everyone, even me. But since I had nothing, since I was nothing, at least I was his. I had to have something, and belonging to Joe was better than nothing. That's what I thought, back then.

He told me how to wear my hair, how to dress, how to walk and how to talk. I was from a small town, so he knew best. My mother and sister came to see me once. Mom said I looked like a tramp. I wished then that I asked her to drive me home with her. I started smoking and drinking. Drugs too. Joe gave me the drugs. He did them, so I did them too. I didn't wonder if it was all wrong. And I never asked where he got his money.

The smartest thing I guess was keeping my job. It always paid shit, but it was something. I almost lost it, though, when the cops came into the nightclub looking for me for questioning. Everyone saw them come in. Real embarrassing. I just told them all of what I'm telling you now. But that was after they took him in, finally . . . I'll get back to the beginning.

Things were good, or almost good, between us. But he could be mean, too. He used to tell me I was stupid, useless, and nothing without him. I knew it was probably true. He said I was only good for sex and serving drinks, and I knew that was true too. I never went beyond high school, and didn't get good grades, so I guess he was right. If I was smart, I would have left him.

But he didn't start beating on me until things got bad for him. I woke up one morning early and he was having an argument with some strange men I never saw before, they were down in the kitchen. I looked out the window and saw all the cars parked out there, expensive ones. Three of them. And the fight was getting loud. I went down to see what was up, and asked what was going on. He turned on me and said, "Bitch! Fuckin' get upstairs!" Then he slapped me. Hard. I fell down. I thought the guys would say something to him, but they all just kept arguing, like I wasn't there. Like I didn't matter. I went upstairs and cried. They all left together. He was gone for hours. He came back and was in a good mood, so I didn't say anything. I didn't want any more problems. I figured, maybe it wouldn't happen again. Yeah, right.

One night, Joe had a party at his place. I wouldn't call it our place. It was all guys, though. If they had girlfriends, they didn't bring them. I should have started to worry when I saw that. They got drunk and stupid, especially Joe. Joe started to brag about how he knocked me around when I got out of line. Sometimes I needed to be slapped around, he said. I kept my mouth shut. One of the guys asked if I was any good in bed, so Joe said, "Why don't you all find out for yourselves." I was like, "What? You gotta be kidding, right?" He said, "Shut up, bitch." And that was it. There were like, I don't remember an exact number, maybe twenty of them. I was shoved on the couch, and there wasn't anything I could do. Joe sat in a chair in the back of the room, laughing about it.

After that night, I wanted to leave Joe. But I had nowhere else to go. The girl I had been rooming with before I met Joe moved in with her boyfriend, and I couldn't go back home. I mean, the last thing I said to my mother was "Fuck off!" so I knew I wouldn't be welcome there. Even if I was, I couldn't admit that she was right, could I? I left home to make something of myself, and I couldn't admit that I had failed. I couldn't tell my friends that I worked with about my problems with Joe, because I had only said good things about him, none of it was true, though. And I couldn't go to the cops. It was 1979, and the cops were all men. I had been walking around town looking like a streetwalker and proud of it. Well, that's probably how I felt then. I know now that I should have just gone home. Back then I thought it would be an isolated incident. That's what I told myself. Every time he did something really cruel, that's what I told myself.

It was only going to get worse.

One night I went to work with a black eye. This other waitress asked if everything was okay, as if she wanted to help me. We weren't on good terms. She kept saying that she only worked there to save up to go to school, and she never slept with any of the customers. She went back to the room she rented and studied. That pissed me off. Who the hell did she think she was? She asked me if I was okay. I told her to get the hell out of my face. She said, "Hey, like I'm just worried about you. That's all." I told her that all that was wrong was that she was just jealous, and to get her own boyfriend. She stopped talking to me after that. I guess now maybe she really wanted to help. Maybe she would have, even if it was just someone to talk to.

My sister called one night before Thanksgiving, and said that Mom wanted to know if I was coming home. She would send my uncle to come pick me up if I was. I couldn't come home. My face was by then black and blue, and I looked like shit. I couldn't let them see that. I told her no, never mind. Forget it.

Thanksgiving was a drunken brawl at Joe's place. At least people were fighting with each other, so no one raped me for Thanksgiving. No one raped me that day, let us now give thanks! There was no turkey, just chips, dip, pretzels, beer, liquor, and coke. Yeah, I mean that kind of coke. This time some men brought their girls, which was okay by me. If there were other girls there, I figured I wouldn't be in trouble.

After a while into the relationship Joe started bringing home girls he found at the bar where I worked. I watched him pick them up. I was just relieved. Some of my friends asked about it. I would say something like, you know, hey, get with it, it's the seventies. We're an open minded couple. I knew that Joe would probably kill me if I was ever with anyone else. So I slept in a chair in the living room when he was upstairs with his new girlfriends. I just didn't care anymore.

Then there was the night Joe got arrested. He called up and asked me to bail him out. I said I had no money. He said, "Stupid bitch, go into the basement, look under the stairs, and get the cash. There's a metal box, under the stairs. Come on. You know how much I love you, baby. Get the cash. Now!" I never knew about the money he had stashed down there.

I should have just grabbed the cash and the Cadillac and all my clothes and took off for parts unknown. There was plenty of cash in the box to keep me for a couple of months while I looked for a better situation. Or I could have brought the coke to the cops. There was coke down there, too. Enough coke that maybe I could have made a profit. But I was nineteen. And pretty stupid. Looking back, I had plenty of opportunities to leave Joe.

Why didn't I? I look back and see all the ways I could have left.

Anyway, I also noticed when I went down into the basement to get the money that it smelled really strange down there, like something died down there. I should have wondered about it, but I didn't.

Why did I stay? Maybe out of stupidity. He did say I was stupid. Maybe I believed I needed him to be someone. I felt I needed someone, even if he was abusive and a drug dealer. Yeah. I finally figured that out. Took me a while, though.

If I was smart, I would have left him in jail and grabbed the money and the car. I really should have. He knew I was too dumb to see a good opportunity. I look back, and see all the ways I could have gotten away. I could have called home, or gone to my uncle, or told the cops, or that poor girl I yelled at, or asked my friends for help, or whatever. I could have wiped him out of his money and drugs, too. Maybe I still deluded myself, thinking he was cool for having all that money and stuff.

It was all right in front of me. I just didn't want to see it, I guess. Today they call it being in denial. Hey, like I said. I was nineteen.

So like an idiot I bailed him out. He was happy, so things were good again between us. I began to actually think he really loved me, so I was happy too. We started sleeping together again. I got pregnant, but I was nervous about telling him, so I didn't. I wanted to wait until he was like you know, in a really good mood. I knew now that he was dealing drugs and into crime. He had guns stashed away too. A lot of guns.

I still thought that being with him made me cool.

Things were going along okay and he was making money again dealing drugs, so he started to seem happy again. There was talk of some people disappearing too, people who knew Joe and maybe double-crossed him some way. Five people who were seen hanging around with Joe in the past had disappeared. Four guys and a girl named Cheryl. Cheryl was the girlfriend before he picked me up in the club. She disappeared a month before he met me. I found that out from the head waitress. She whispered that to me when she saw me in the break room looking at a newspaper. There was a picture of Cheryl, and it read like this, "What happened to Cheryl Robertson?" There was a picture of her in the paper. She was young, and pretty, and blonde. She almost kind of looked like me.

I didn't think much about it. Joe had good lawyers, and felt sure of getting out of trouble. He had money, and bought me a few things. I knew he was bad, but I couldn't believe he would kill someone. Not Joe.

I must have been as dumb as he said I was.

Like, all around me there were warning signs of things that I ignored. I ignored that he told me what to do all the time. I ignored it that he hit me. I ignored it that he had guns and did drugs. I ignored it that he had money and no one seemed to ever say where it came from. I tried to ignore that he let his friends use me. I ignored that he had other women.

I could have told him "No" that night when he wanted me to sleep with him. I mean, I didn't have to. I could have avoided all this trouble. I could have ignored him when he said to come to his place, that first night I went home with him.

But I thought I needed to be with someone in order to be someone, so I stayed and I bailed him out of jail that night.

He was good to me for a while.

Then came bad news. There was a witness somewhere, someone who said that she saw him fighting with Cheryl in the bar the night she disappeared. And more bad news. Some neighbors saw the cars belonging to the men he was fighting with on the morning he hit me. And one of them, the Lincoln, was the same car that was later on hauled out of the lake.

And it was getting obvious. I had to say that I was pregnant.

Cops called me in for questioning. They wanted me maybe for a witness. And no one was sure if I was involved with his crimes, like helping him or not. They also suspected I was a prostitute. Word of the gang-bang got around, and I was the subject of everyone's jokes. People said I was a slut. When I was working, I heard customers whispering behind my back.

The cops thought I was part of it. I had to finally tell the truth.

I was scared, because I was carrying his baby.

He knew the cops wanted me to talk. So, now get this, he bought a big diamond and asked me to marry him, if I kept quiet. "You know how much I love you, baby. We've been through so much together."

I don't know what happened to me that night. Something inside turned on, like an electric light switching on. I saw things now, the way I never saw them before. Images flashed in my head. The picture of Cheryl in the paper, the black and white photo of the Lincoln being hauled out of the lake, the photos of his "known associates," some of whom were missing or found dead.

And I remembered, especially, all his friends raping me that night.

"Joe, what happened to Cheryl?"

"The bitch ran off with some strange guy, that's all, baby. Now how 'bout it? You know how much you mean to me."

He figured that if I married him everything would be okay, I wouldn't testify, and I would keep quiet. I put the ring on my finger, but I didn't say anything to him; I never said I would marry him. I kept my mouth shut. But all of a sudden, all this stuff was going on inside my head. I had more than just myself to think about now. It was no longer about having the image of being his girlfriend, or saying I was his. I had to think about little Joe now. And I sure as hell didn't want him to grow up to be like his dad. I left him, saying I was on my way to work, because they needed me early. But I went to the police instead.

I told them everything I knew. Everything.

The cops arranged for me to stay somewhere safe until the trial. They wanted to bring him down, plus the rest of the drug ring. He wasn't the big boss, it turned out. He was just a part of the bigger picture. The FBI was in this too. It went really deep. Of course, I was too stupid to know about that stuff. I didn't know names, or how much money was floating around; but I knew faces. Joe had pretty much kept me ignorant. Maybe he wanted me as his girlfriend because I was in fact nothing but a stupid nineteen year old girl.

But I was about to grow up, and get smart, real fast.

The baby would come soon. Newspaper reporters had my picture taken from the neck up. It wasn't so fashionable then to be a single mother, like it is now. I was pretty, and it made a great story. The brave, beautiful heroine who brought down the big bad mob. Yeah, right. I was scared in that courtroom. I cried. I just wanted to go home, I wanted my mother. But it was too late. My mother wanted nothing to do with me anymore.

The baby was coming, and I needed a safe home for Joe Junior. I was sick of being afraid. Image wasn't important to me anymore, not like it was before. I wasn't going to let myself be in denial about it all anymore, either. I had to admit to myself that I was in an abusive relationship, and that I didn't really have it all together, like I wanted people to think. I was nothing but a victim. But we're only victims if we let ourselves become victims. Remember that. It sounds like a cliché, but it but that's how it is.

My relationship with my family is still ruined. My mother, still after all these years, won't speak to me. My sister went on to school and became a nurse. I haven't seen her in years. My uncle died of a heart attack, and they never told me. I never got a chance to go to the funeral.

Joe Junior dropped out of high school despite my yelling at him to stick with it and do something like trade school. He got arrested a few times, nothing serious, just assault and stuff. I haven't seen him in years either. He disappeared one day, took a few clothes in a duffle bag and just left. He didn't say where to. He just sort of left. Got in his car, and went.

The money is gone too. The cops took what was left of it as evidence, they said. It was a lot of cash. I could have lived well on that for a while. Maybe paid for some kind of school for myself. But the cash is gone now. Then they dug up the basement, and found the rest of the bodies they were looking for all those years while they were investigating. They found Cheryl down there too.

So here I am, at the top of my career. A waitress working late nights in a bar. Yeah, right now I'm talking to you, remembering the best days of my life. Give me another cigarette, honey, will yah?

But I guess I walked right into it. I should have left him, but I stayed. I had something to prove to everyone else, so I stayed. I had to prove I was a mature woman, that I could handle it, and in control of my life. I wasn't controlling my life. Joe was. And I couldn't handle it.

And I had a lot of opportunities to escape, but I never did until it was almost too late. In the end, only the cops would help me, and it was only because they needed a witness.

Why am I telling you all this stuff? Because I see girls like you all the time. Young, pretty, thinking you're just so smart. Listen. Guys don't say nice things to you because they actually care about you. They just want what they want. Of course, back then, I wanted whatever I could get, too. I wish I could go back to my younger self, tell myself to get my dumb ass back on the bus and head back home and become anything but what I am now. I could have gone to school, or something. I could have done something with my life, instead of all this.

Listen, honey. Don't make the mistakes I made. Go to the community college, go to hairdresser school, do anything, just don't let someone like that completely take over your life like I did. Don't let him start telling you how to dress, how to walk and how to talk. And don't get into drugs and do shit like that to impress him or his friends either.

Because it is nothing but a trap. Believe me, I know.

And if you are in a bad relationship now, get free any way you can. That's why I always tell this story. Because stuff like that happens all the time, everywhere.

Face the hard truth. Women are nothing to men like Joe. There are good men out there. But you don't find them around here. Good men don't drink, gamble, and pick up girls twenty years younger and make them into whores. The good ones are the ones I thought were dull. Why? I don't know. Maybe they just weren't cool. But now I know that cool is stupid. No one will take care of you but you. If you expect someone to take care of you because you are pretty, you are wrong. Go to school while you still can, and make something of yourself. That's what I wish I had done, when I was your age.

And you know, I really need a damn drink right now.

End of the Line!

Don Talbot grew more and more frustrated while sitting in the vast waiting room, still just waiting for what seemed like eternity. Men like him should not have to wait. He was someone important, and he should have been moved to the front of the line, before everyone else. He couldn't understand why he was put at the end of the line, like a common ordinary person, just because he was just as dead as all the others there. Once more, he looked up and looked around. The waiting area went on and on and on, and he saw the vast numbers of formerly living people, from everywhere, all around the world, all ethnic groups and nationalities. And they all had to wait their turn.

"They're doing the people who died in the 60's now," the kid sitting next to him said. "I think they're going to call me soon. I hope so. I've been sitting her since . . . I dunno . . . almost half a century, I think."

Don looked at the young man beside him. He wore a uniform, and Don guessed he had served in Vietnam. That's why he was there, sitting next to him, waiting with him to be processed.

"I shouldn't have to wait like this," Don said, angrily. "I was somebody. I was a CEO. A billionaire. I had a private jet." Suddenly he smirked to himself. "Well, that's how I died. The private jet went down over the ocean. I was on my way to check out an island I was going to buy. Anyway," he said to the young deceased soldier, "I shouldn't have to wait like this. I was important. I owned big companies. I created jobs. I was somebody."

57

"Yeah, Mister, yeah. We're all just dead here. We all have to wait until they send us to the next place, wherever that is going to be. I dunno, Mister. A guy ahead of me, he died in a car crash after drinking all night long, and he's gone on to the Big Wherever now; but he said to me, you either get Heaven, Hell, or reincarnation. Once you finally get to that desk up there," he pointed, "Way up there, at the big desk, they check your records. They keep a file on everybody. They see what you made of your life, and then they assign you out of here. You go on the next place. I'm not worried, though. I never got a chance to shoot anyone. They got me first. So I didn't get to break that 'thou shalt not kill' thing they tell you about in Sunday school."

"Well," Don growled, "They review your file, huh?" He stood up and straightened out his suit jacket, "I'm going up there, then. I did a lot with my life. I wasn't just some loser like everybody else. I'm going to demand they put me up at the top of their list!"

"Hey, no, Mister!" the soldier said as Don began to saunter slowly toward the big desk where souls were reviewed before being moved along, "You gotta wait your turn!"

Don ignored the young man and kept going, pushing others in the crowd aside, and not bothering to even mumble "excuse me" when shoving a blind man with his guide dog who had both been struck down by a city bus. Finally, after what seemed like walking miles, he got to the desk, which when he got up close he saw that it appeared to be like a reception desk at a hotel—a cheap dump of a hotel, he thought to himself. There were only three people there sitting at the desk, slowly working to process everyone, reviewing, of all things, normal looking manila file folders filled with actual paperwork. He pushed aside the elderly woman who was standing there to demand attention and cleared his throat.

"Don't you people know who I am?" He looked directly down at an attractive woman sitting at the large ornate mahogany desk. In front of her was a golden nameplate that said "SaraBeth: Head of Central Processing." The other two at the desk had gold nameplates that simply said, "Joshua" and "Michael."

"What?" said the Head of Central Processing, who had been assisting the elderly woman when Don shoved her aside to get ahead, "Sir! This lady is not quite done yet, can't you see? Go back to sit down and wait to be called, please!"

"I said, don't you people know who I am? I'm Don Talbot, CEO of Talbot Industries! Billionaire! I built skyscrapers! I created companies! Everyone knows me! How could you people not know who I am?"

"Sir," the woman at the desk answered, "Your wealth does not matter here. Now go sit until you are called, please."

"I should not have to wait at the end of the line!" he roared. Everyone stared at him. "I am Don Talbot! I was in the news all the time! I even ran for the Senate! Don't you people even watch TV up here?! I was rich, I was a great guy, and women all loved me! I had real estate, I owned casinos, I owned an airline, I—"

"Go! To! The! End! Of the line!" the Head of Central Processing stood up and loudly commanded, "Right now, Mr. Talbot! And yes, we do know who you are! Of course you're famous, or should I say, well known, up here! Now sit down!" Suddenly she turned back to the elderly woman, "You can go upstairs, ma'am, you're all set. I'll just expedite your paperwork. Go on, now, Mrs. Cranston," she pointed toward the direction the lady was to go, "Go down that hallway, first elevator on the right. That elevator only goes up. Oh, and about your question that you had earlier. I had Michael here check our main computer. Yes! All of your cats will be waiting for you up there. The reason you don't see many animals in the Eternal Waiting Room is because most animals just go straight to Heaven. I'll ask Joshua to call ahead, and your pets will meet you when you get off the elevator. Okay?"

The old lady smiled and then happily shuffled off.

Now, once again SaraBeth glared at the CEO Don Talbot, "And why are you still standing in front of this desk?"

"Because I demand attention! Now! I am not going to wait around for eternity, like all these losers! You will have me assigned to wherever I am supposed to go, this minute!"

"Oh! Is that it, Mr. Talbot? Well, if you want it that way, sir. In fact, you're so well known, I don't even have to look at your file!"

The two men sitting next to her at the desk stopped their work and watched as she picked up her phone. Joshua laughed slightly, and then went back to the person he was assisting.

"Hello?" SaraBeth said into the phone, "Mr. Scratch? Can you send someone up here, please? Like, now? Yeah. I'm sorry. I know you're all so busy down there, but we've got Mr. Talbot. You know, Don Talbot? Yes, the Don Talbot. Talbot Industries. Billionaire Don Talbot! He's here early. I didn't check his paperwork yet, so I don't know why he's here, but I'm pretty sure he's yours, anyway. Okay? Thanks, Mr. Scratch. Bye! He's waiting for yah!"

"Good," snarled Talbot, "I'll just wait right here!"

"Oh, it won't be long," said Joshua.

Michael shot him a look and went back to his paperwork and mumbled, "Okay. Next."

Suddenly a man walked directly through the long line toward Don Talbot. He was a handsome young man with an expensive suit, polished fine Italian leather shoes, and a silk tie, "Mr. Talbot?"

"Yes! I am Don Talbot."

The handsome young man held out his hand and Don Talbot shook it firmly, "Pleased to meet you, sir. You're very well-known and admired where I come from."

"Well, finally, I'm getting the respect I deserve!"

"Please come with me, Mr. Talbot."

"Certainly." Finally, Don was going somewhere. As he followed the young man, those who had been waiting for probably decades gazed coldly at him.

"Come with me, Mr. Talbot, this way, please, we're taking this elevator here," and the young man led Don into a large elevator and hit the button.

"I'm glad finally someone is behaving with decency toward me, young man! I deserve respect! I did a lot with my life. I'm not just some loser who assembled widgets all day!" he smiled at the young man, but strangely, the man in the fine suit did not smile back.

"Did you build homeless shelters?" the strange man asked.

"Why, no . . . No! Why should I?"

61

"Did you feed the hungry?"

"Nope. That's not my responsibility. Who cares? Why do you ask?" Suddenly, it felt warm in the elevator, and Don noticed the sensation of downward motion. "Say? I think you hit the wrong button, there . . . What?" Don looked at the control panel. "This thing only has one button that says "D" on it. What the hell is going on? Why are we going down?"

The young man finally smiled, "Actually, Don, the D stands for Damnation."

Crossing the Bridge

This time Earl swore to himself he was going to do it. He was finally going to jump, he said to himself. But he looked down and the river looked dark and cold and filthy with the city's pollution. But he was going to finally do it. This was it; he was going to finish it, this time.

He tried to make the jump last week and looked down into the dark cold water and felt sick and was a damn coward and walked away. He tried it again a few days ago and couldn't do it then, either.

He held onto the steel of the bridge and moved closer toward the edge. A few more inches and he'd be falling, speeding fast into the water where he would drown his miserable life. He moved closer to the edge and was finally ready to let go, to lean forward and dive in.

"Hey, Earl!"

He turned to look behind him. There stood a young girl in faded jeans and a simple T-shirt, with mouse brown hair, and probably no more than nineteen or twenty, "Do I know you?"

"No. No, Earl. You don't know me," she said. "But I know you. And you're seeing me because you're so close to the edge right now."

"Who the hell are you? And why the hell don't you just leave me alone? Can't you see I'm busy trying to accomplish something here today?"

"Who the hell am I? I'm Margie. But that's not important. I just want to talk to you. I want to talk to you about what you're planning to do, Earl."

"What business is it of yours, Margie?"

"Earl, once you cross over that bridge, there is no going back," she said, sounding very serious and definite.

Earl wondered if she was crazier than he was right now, "Look, girl, I am not crossing the bridge, I am planning to jump off it. Get it? Now go away, will yah?"

"That's not what I mean. And of course I know you're planning to jump. Because when you die, you cross over and that will be it. You'll regret it, Earl. You'll regret the missed chances and opportunities you left behind. You'll regret leaving the people who mattered to you, before you could tell them that you loved them. You'll never be able to come back to say, 'I love you.' I know what I'm talking about, Earl."

He looked away from her, and once again looked down into the river below. He thought for a few minutes, saying nothing, and then, "Yeah. I dunno. My life isn't going too well right now. Lost my job. The repo man stole my car. Got a foreclosure notice in the mail. Can't take much more, Margie, whatever you say your name is," he turned to look at her, but then she was gone. He looked around to see if she was walking away in disgust, but she was nowhere. There was no one around. He was alone. Completely alone, "What the hell?"

But he came down from where he intended to make the jump from, deciding maybe to give life one more day, or one more chance. Maybe he would get a new job soon, and maybe he'd manage to hang on to his house. He could ride the bus until he could afford another car. Maybe . . . maybe it would all work out? But he would never know if he did make the jump.

He started walking, heading for home. On the way, he stopped at a coffee shop, deciding that coffee and a donut might clear his head, if only just a little bit. And that was another problem he had been having: With being out of work, he couldn't afford groceries sometimes. He knew he had a few bucks in his pocket, probably his last few bucks, but enough for a coffee and a donut.

In the coffee shop he sat at a table in the corner, alone, wanting to just be by himself to collect his miserable thoughts and reflect on his miserable life. He was just thirty and since he lost his job he was probably about to lose everything. He didn't know if things would get better, but the girl was right. Once he did it, there would be no going back.

On the next table there was a newspaper. He reached for it. He almost dropped it when he saw the black and white photograph on the front page. It was Margie.

The headline read, *Body Found in River Identified*.

"What?" And that was all he could say. The girl's name was Margery Cavendish, age 19. She had drowned, and possibly committed suicide. The body had been in the river for probably over a week, and was in poor condition, and therefore hard to identify. Her parents were interviewed, the mother very tearful, "She was upset about things, we still don't know what. She ran out the door one day, and didn't come back. I wish she could come back, just so we could tell her that we love her."

He put the paper down and remembered what the girl had said, "I know what I'm talking about. Once you cross over that bridge, there is no going back."

He finished his coffee, folded up the paper, and took it with him when he left.

Blood Money

So you say you need to make some extra money? Yeah. I can help fix you up with some good clients. There's a lot of cash to be made doing this. It's like I have my own part time business. I'm even thinking of having business cards made up. The problem is, I can't keep up with all the customers. There's too many of them these days. And I keep telling yah, it's not as bad as yah think, okay? First, let me tell yah all about how I got into this line of work, so you won't think I'm some kind of psycho.

It all started the night I got kicked out of my apartment. I hadn't been able to pay the rent for a few months. The company I worked for closed its doors, I was out of work, and the unemployment ran out. Happens to a lot of people, especially these days. Had only like five bucks in my pocket, and the clothes on my back. There was like twenty in my savings, I remember. The phone was dead the week before, and I was okay with that, because that way I didn't have to listen to the collectors who kept calling me. The landlord wasn't even letting me back in to get my stuff, which was probably illegal. I didn't have much anyway, clothes, a few beers in the fridge, a cheap TV, CD's, an old computer, a few pairs of blue jeans, sneakers: the usual stuff an apartment dweller has. So I landed on the street with five bucks and no food.

I checked in at the shelter. The people at the desk said they were full. They sent me to the soup kitchen, though, which was at least a meal. Next I sat on a bench under a streetlight and wondered what the hell I was gonna do.

I had no family locally, none that would take me in, anyway. I thought about stuff that I had read about people who end up on the streets. They end up either getting knifed by some crackhead, or if they live, they end up selling their ass. I did not want to be knifed, and for sure I did not want to sell my ass. I actually began to wonder how low I would sink if I got hungry enough, cold enough, scared enough. It was November and I had only my leather jacket. It was midnight, it was starting to snow, and I was getting miserable.

Then I heard this voice, "Do you want to make some money?" I was relieved that it was a lady's voice, and not some guy. I looked up, and there was a black Cadillac. The blonde lady in the Cadillac wore a mink coat, matching fur hat, diamond necklace and I am like, oh honey, take me for a ride! She was drop dead gorgeous. There was someone in the seat next to her, too—a blonde and a brunette. The brunette wore a white fox coat. "Want some company, ladies?" I asked, and made a big friendly smile.

"Open the door for him." Said the blonde. She reminded me of a film star from the forties. Something about her seemed old fashioned, yet sophisticated.

"Oh Clarisse!" The other one giggled, then said, "You're not serious? Are you?"

The door opened. So I got in. Looked like I was about to sell my ass. But the customers were the kind I like, at least. They looked good, they smelled good—hell, I had never seen two women who looked that clean in a very long time. I got in the backseat of the car and sat behind the ladies.

"I'm Clarisse. This is Rachel."

I looked at Rachel; she reminded me of Jackie Kennedy.

"And I'm Jake! Hello, lovely ladies!" I was new at this routine, and I supposed these two girls could probably tell.

"Would you like to earn some money?" said Clarisse.

I decided to be honest. "Okay, girls. Right now, yeah, I could use some money." And I probably had a desperate look on my face too, which is probably why they pulled their car over next to the bench I sat on.

"Oh, but it's not really what you think," said Rachel, "You see, Clarisse and I, well, we're—"

"We're vampiresses!" said lovely Clarisse. And she smiled when she said it, saying it with the same happy tone of voice you would hear as if some girl said "We're stewardesses!" And when she smiled, I could see her teeth. Her sharp teeth.

"Huh?" It took a moment to get over my shock. I sat there, in the back of the Cadillac, staring at them both. I wasn't sure if I should believe it or not, but somehow I knew it was true. What kept me seated was the fact that Clarisse was in the process of opening her little expensive designer pocketbook and pulling out this thick wad of cash. I had never seen so much damn money in front of me in my life before.

Rachel looks at me and says, "Oh you don't need to worry, Jake. We don't kill people like you see on TV. We usually live off animal blood. We buy it from slaughterhouses. But sometimes we—especially Clarisse here—sometimes it's nice to have something fresh and warm and alive for a change."

68

Clarisse kept counting out, "How about five hundred? Is that enough, Jake?" She smiled again, "We can drive to my place, or I can just come sit in the backseat with you?"

I thought about it. My head was spinning but I kept my eyes on the cash. Then I said, "You're not going to drink it all, right?" I was like, hey, I need some leftover for me, girls.

"No!" Says Clarisse, "Of course not! I wouldn't want to harm you. Just enough to enjoy some of your blood, Jake."

And then Rachel pipes up, "And it will be just Clarisse. If both of us had you tonight, you'd be weakened by it. And that's just not ethical."

Sheesh. I'm about to sell my ass—or actually, blood— to a rich vampiress, and these two are discussing ethics. I thought about it, and I realized—my only other alternative might be to actually sell my ass, which would be a lot more degrading. Yeah. It really would be. I even began to wonder which alternative would actually hurt more.

"Okay," I mumbled weakly.

"Yes?" Clarisse almost looked happily surprised. "Well, all right." She opened the door to get out of the driver's seat and stepped out of the car to come into the back seat. I guess vampiresses just have too much class to just climb over.

I got worried then. I wondered if I might be found dead and drained on the side of the road the next morning. But then I could be found dead anyway, since I was now officially homeless street scum. Only this way, she might keep her promise and leave me alive with five hundred bucks.

She came into the back seat while Rachel took the wheel and pulled the car off the road to park it.

"Don't be nervous," said Clarisse.

"Oh, like, hell no! I'm not nervous." Like, yeah. I was.

So she sat herself right next to me. Next thing I know she's undoing the collar of my shirt. I felt myself shaking but I shut up and thought about the five hundred bucks and hoped to be alive when it was all over so I could just get the money.

She moved in close, and I felt this little nick, like two needles piercing my skin. Then when the blood began to flow she withdrew her teeth and pressed her lips to my throat and quietly drank. I closed my eyes and tried not to be scared. And then I realized something, which was actually a strange thing to realize in this situation—that I'd never been this close to a real mink coat before.

She held onto me with an almost tight embrace while she drank from my throat, and I could tell she was enjoying it. As time went on, I began to enjoy it too. It felt almost like a prolonged intense kiss. After a while I began to sink into this dark oblivion of peacefulness and warmth. I forgot about my problems. I just relaxed and let go and let it happen.

But then she let go of me and suddenly I felt cold. I didn't want her to let go; I wanted her to keep on doing what she was doing. It was like part of me had gone to sleep and I didn't want to wake up. I felt her stuff something into the pocket of my leather jacket. But now the five hundred didn't seem to matter that much anymore. My eyes were closed, and I felt too weak to open them, but I could hear them talk.

"Did you take too much?" it was Rachel in the front seat.

"Don't think so. His pulse is still strong. Maybe he hasn't been eating. He's awfully thin, isn't he?" Clarisse was right. The unemployment had run out, and it was tough to pay for both rent and groceries. "Other than that, it's great to finally have a meal that's not from a refrigerator." She actually sighed. "And he's sort of cute too." I felt her fingertips run along my wound, caressing my throat.

"Well, either way, I think you're paying him too much," Rachel again. And I wanted her to shut the hell up.

"Yes, well, he looks like he could use it. I don't think he'd be on a bench if he didn't need the cash. If he had a home, he'd be there right now. Wouldn't he?"

"What are you going to do with him now, Clarisse, since you're apparently done with him?"

"Let's find a hotel or something. Drop him off. He's waking up now anyway."

"Why don't you get his cell phone number, if he has a cell phone. In case he wants to make more easy money?" This time I was glad Rachel wouldn't shut up.

My eyes slowly opened and I was alone in the backseat. Clarisse was in the passenger seat and Rachel was driving the Cadillac. I looked out the window and we had pulled up next to a cheap motel. The girls dropped me off. I walked a little unsteady, but I was basically okay. Clarisse asked if I was all right. I assumed I was. I was alive, I was about to spend the rest of the night in a bed instead of on the streets, and I had five hundred bucks in my pocket. Yeah. I was okay.

I shuffled into the motel. There was this kid half asleep at the desk. I asked what the cheapest room was, then I noticed the sign. Help Wanted. As I wandered off to bed, I thought about that.

In the morning, I had breakfast at the fast food place next to the motel, and then went to ask about the job. It was janitorial, but it was a job. I started work there, and worked out a deal to stay in the room. Eventually I got a desk job. It doesn't pay much, but I have extra income, any time I want it. Any time I want nice clothes, a new CD player, stuff like that, and I'm saving for a car.

Hold on a minute. I gotta answer my cell phone. I think it's a customer.

Twenty Sixty Eight

The ship's engine was a constant drone in the background while he stared vacantly out into the night's darkness, gazing silently at the endlessness of the sea, the cold damp wind ruffling his hair.

"What will you do now?" The girl's voice came suddenly from behind him.

He turned to look at her, her straw colored hair waving in the night breeze, blue eyes wide and almost sad, her face almost as pale as his. She seemed to have been watching him, following him since the incident.

"What will you do?" she asked again, "Now that your supply is gone?"

"I don't really know." He looked away from her and back out into the darkness of the ocean, "Starve, I suppose."

"Do you know who's responsible?"

"Does it matter? No one on this ship trusts me. I would be grateful if they don't toss me overboard in the morning. Or worse." The small refrigerator in his cabin had been emptied by persons unknown. Whoever they were, they had a key, suggesting it had been a member of the crew. But why? His first conclusion was that someone wanted to start trouble for him, cause him to lose control of his thirst. Or perhaps it was for revenge? He looked at her sad face again, "It's late. You should go to bed."

"No. Let me help you."

He didn't respond, simply continued to stare out at the water.

"You protected me from those raging drunks. So let me help you."

"You don't owe me anything. And you look too fragile. What are you? Ninety-five pounds at the most, I would guess."

"I do owe you. And you'd be careful. Won't you? I just know you would."

He looked away, and struggled to ignore her.

"Come on," she took his ivory white hand, "Not here. Someone might see. And besides, I'm cold."

She walked along and he followed her almost reluctantly. Once back in his cabin he gazed at her in the darkness, knowing that although he could see her clearly, she could barely see him at all, "I don't even know your name?"

"Emily. Emily Davenport. And you're Roderick Murray? Isn't that correct?"

"Roderick Moroy," he correctly gently, "Most people get it wrong. It's the Americanized version of my family's Eastern European name, but never mind. I see information travels quickly on this poor excuse for a ship. I suppose you'd want the light on?"

"No. Don't bother, Roderick. No. Before I got onboard, I read all about your lecture series, 'Vampires: Myth and Reality.' I was thinking about attending. And then I saw you. There were, the vampire rights activist, right here, on this boat. I recognized you from the picture in the magazine article. And, well, . . . I-I guess this is as real as it gets." Her brief stammer revealed a small amount of fear. "I'm glad you're onboard with me, especially, well, because—"

He interrupted her excited speech, "You don't owe me anything, really, Emily. You can leave if you want. Or maybe you're like many people I've met while traveling, who wonder what it would be like to get up close and personal? With a vampire?"

She removed her woolen scarf and came towards him, "Are you hungry or not?"

He took a hold of her thin shoulders, "Last chance to change your mind."

She said nothing. He bent to her throat. She quivered slightly when she felt her flesh pierced. Her legs went weak but he held on to her. She sighed as he drank gently from the open wound.

She awakened on his bed with a blanket over her, "You passed out. But I really didn't take much."

She sat up, "Oh. I'm just a little light headed. That's all."

"You're all right, then?"

"I . . . I think so."

"It won't stop this terrible hunger, but it will keep me from getting weak. Thank you, Emily. I'll make contact with some people before I disembark, and they'll come for me, with a delivery, packed in ice. So soon you won't have to worry about me."

She looked at him in the semi-darkness. He sat in a chair on the other side of the small room, "This will also irritate my fundamentalist parents. I'm a runaway, you know."

"Then I certainly hope they don't find the both of us together like this. We're both in enough trouble with the other passengers hunting after you and the crew plotting against me. And how old did you say you were?"

"Don't worry. They'll never find me. And I didn't say how old I was. I'm twenty-two. But I ran away from home, just like a delinquent. And I guess I'm what people would call sheltered. They had a wedding planned for me, only I didn't know about it until a few weeks ago. I was supposed to marry someone I had never met. So I took all the money my wicked sinful grandmother left for me— she was wicked because she went to college and had a job out in the real world, and good girls just don't do things like that—and I packed a bag, and bought a ticket on this horrible old junk of a cargo ship. I didn't have much time to make plans, but I guess I plan to land somewhere, get a place to stay, and get a job, and go to school, and just do something with my life. Something besides being someone's third wife and mother to the fifteen kids he already has. I don't know. I'll do anything. Be a waitress, or go to hairdresser school. I still don't know what I'll do. And maybe I want to travel, see the world. But I guess I'm sort of traveling now, even though I'm just seeing the inside of this ship and trying to avoid getting raped. Kind of ironic since I left home to avoid being sort of raped."

He waited for her to finally finish what was apparently a combination of her life's story and an explanation for her behavior, "Well, Emily, I bought a ticket on this horrible cargo ship because the jets have been grounded for yet another supposed terrorist threat. Also it's a rather anonymous way to travel, I suppose. I'm travelling and I can't be held up. I'm one hundred and twenty two, even though they say I look about thirty, and for all the time that I've lived I've seen that the majority of people do little else but start wars and blow things up. Sad but true. It's good that your wicked grandmother was such a bad influence on you. You deserve to make your own choices in life. And as they used to say so many decades ago, you go girl."

"They used to say that? When? I bet it was the sixties." She grew excited, "I wish I lived in the sixties, so I could run away and become a hippie."

"No. It was slightly more recently than that. And maybe you wouldn't want to be a hippie. They didn't do very much besides get high."

"High?" She was confused.

"You know. Like drugged up high. They would get so drugged up, some of them believed they could fly, and they would leap off a roof. I stood on a sidewalk one night and saw a kid not much younger than me land on the pavement. People were shouting, 'Don't do it, man!' But he yelled, 'Watch, I can fly!' And then he jumped. That was how I remember the sixties. Kids running away to join cults, getting high and dancing naked and barking at the moon . . ."

Her eyes widened, "Really?"

"Maybe you wouldn't really want to be a hippie, Emily. I suppose they had fun for a while, but some of them were rather useless."

"Oh well. I guess I'll just be a runaway, then. I'm running away from a cult, I think. Or maybe I'm wrong. Maybe my parents are right, and I'm going to hell."

"Maybe you are running away from a cult. I don't know of many people who arrange marriages in this century," he hesitated and then said, "Well, if you're going to be a runaway, then you need to learn some survival skills. First, never tell anyone you have money with you. You're lucky that most vampires in general don't steal. Hide it very well. And don't speak about it to anyone. Next you need to know to avoid rowdy drunks. You realize that now, I'm sure. Try not to be alone and if you are, then always watch your back."

She yawned, "I guess maybe I am more than a little sheltered. I was home-schooled, and was only allowed to have friends from our church. I've never been away from home much before. I got on this boat to get as far away as I can. My parents told me that everyone in the outside world is evil. But I never really believed it."

"Well, it's late." It was nearly dawn. He closed the curtains around the small porthole. "Stay here as long as you like. I'll sleep on the floor." He went to fetch himself an extra pillow and blanket from the closet.

She lay back on the bed again, "If I'm not going to be a hippie, then I can cut my hair. My parents' church didn't let women cut their hair. It would be yards long if I didn't snip inches off it in secret," her sleepy voice became a whisper, "And I want to buy some regular clothes, like the kind I see girls wear in magazines." Slowly she drifted into the darkness of sleep. "I just realized. You don't sleep in a coffin."

"None of us really do. That's just something from movies. And I was wondering what was up with that old fashioned calico print dress and the white socks," he recalled she wore a trench coat wherever she went, as if to hide her lack of a normal wardrobe, "I thought you said you read up all about us."

"Well," she admitted sheepishly, "It was just one article. I wasn't allowed to read a lot of things that weren't approved by our church, you know, growing up."

"I understand, then. For the record, most of us depend on animal blood, so don't worry. You're not associating with a murderer. Have a good rest, Emily. You can tell me more at dusk. Or ask more questions about my people, if you like."

It was hours later, dusk; and the engine was silent. But he could hear the small television. Each cabin had one, he supposed, but he had never bothered to turn it on. It was the first thing he noticed when he awakened. The next thing he noticed was the hard surface of the floor he was on. And then he remembered, "Emily?" He sat up slowly, feeling stiff from a day on the floor.

"They're looking for me."

"What?"

"It's on TV. They're looking for me. I don't want to be a celebrity. I just want to run away and disappear!"

"You're on . . . do they know where you are?" He stood up, ran his thin pale fingers through his dark hair.

She shut it off, "N-no. They don't have a clue. The news said I had mysteriously disappeared, before I was able to marry the man I dearly love, which is unusual that they say that, since I only met him twice. He was on TV, saying, 'Please! Whoever you are! Please bring her back!' And the whole church is praying night and day for my safe return! I don't want to go back, Roderick. I don't! I'll jump overboard!"

"Don't you think they might be worried about you?"

"No. Not really. I think they want the bride price that they would get when I'm sent to my arranged marriage. That's what they're really worried about."

"Bride price? Your family must be involved with a pretty strange group. I see. Well, it won't do much good to jump overboard, Emily. We've docked, so the water is shallow. You'll either be seen, or just wash up on the beach and get caught and sent back home to face your parents. We've got to find a way to smuggle you out."

"How? Do you have a plan?"

He hesitated, "Not yet. Look, I need to make a call. Just hang on. Don't panic." He went to where his leather jacket was hung over a chair and took out his phone from the pocket. "Hello? Yeah. Ralph, it's me. The ship has come in. Look, we . . . I had some trouble. My supply is gone. Some idiots came in when I left my room and tossed it all out. Can someone make a delivery? Fast? Good. Thanks, Ralph. I owe you one."

She was curious, "Who's that?"

He put the phone away, "Whenever we travel, we let others of our kind know where we are in case we need help. It comes in handy. And cell phones just speed up the process. Technology has helped us network better than ever before."

A tear drifted down her cheek, "W-what will I do?"

"I don't know. But don't worry, Emily. You're not getting married anytime soon. Not if I can help it. I just have to think of something."

He met Ralph where he had parked his car by the dock. As soon as Ralph opened the trunk of his car,

Roderick reached into the ice filled cooler and grabbed a bottle, "I can't thank you enough for being so fast."

Ralph smirked, "Don't you want to microwave it?"

He drank it down. "When you're starving, who the hell cares?"

"What happened, Roderick?"

"Idiots tossed it all overboard when I left my cabin. Probably trying to provoke an incident. Why else?" He was silent a moment and reached for another bottle, "Listen, Ralph. I need help with another problem." He looked around and lowered his voice, "Have you seen the news report on the missing girl?"

"What missing girl?"

"Damn. This is gonna be a hell of a long night." Quietly, hoping no one nearby would hear, he explained.

"Oh hell. This is gonna be a real pain in the—"

"Yeah. Right. Look, Ralph. We can't just send her back to that damn cult. She says they're forcing her to marry some guy. And what do you think they'll do to her if they find out she's been with someone like me?"

"I know. I know. But I don't know what to do either. It would look real bad, you know, Roderick, if they found her in your room, you know, with two holes in her."

"Yeah," he smirked, "I suppose it might look bad. That's another reason to sneak her out. Besides she needs help. She's really sheltered. She wouldn't last long on her own." He told Ralph all he knew about her, which was not much besides what she had told him. "She's very trusting, though. Poor kid. She read a little about us. Seemed surprised to learn we don't sleep in a..."

"Well, what are you going to do about it?"

"You still hang out with that girl the hairdresser? The one who wants to become a fashion designer?"

"Yeah? Oh crap. I think I know what you're planning."

"Call her on your phone, Ralph. Get her down here. Now."

"Emily?" He entered the cabin carrying the large plastic container that Ralph brought in the back of his car. It was dark; the television was off. Then he saw her, sitting alone in the corner, "Are you all right?"

"Yeah. I think . . . I think someone tried the door. The handle shook. I shut the light out and stuff. But maybe they were looking for you."

"I think people are out to get the both of us on this ship." He put the box down and quietly began putting bottles into the small refrigerator. "Well, okay look, I have an idea. And I don't think you're going to like it. But it might be the only way you'll leave this ship without being noticed."

"W-what do you mean?"

"Well, I just talked to Ralph out on the dock. He knows someone who maybe can help you."

"Help me? How?"

"If you walk off this ship, you're going to be seen."

"So, how can your friend help me?" she didn't understand.

He sat down on the flat, uncomfortable bed, "Emily," he exhaled slowly, "You know you've been a little sheltered. The way you do your hair, that old fashioned dress—"

"I wasn't allowed to dress any other way. We had to dress in a way approved by our church. But maybe I want to have some new clothes, too, when I figure out where I'm going."

"Well, you know what? Ralph will be back and he'll bring a friend of his. You might like Ralph, because a long time ago, he was one of those hippies you're so fascinated with. He even got knocked over the head by cops while marching for peace, when he was still able to walk in the sun. When he recovered, we both took a road trip. I've known him that long. That's what people did then. It was 1968, exactly one hundred years ago. People back then grew their hair long to rebel against society, just like you're planning to cut your hair to rebel against your parents. We got ourselves an old VW bus, and wandered the country aimlessly, just to see America, he said. But actually the trip we took was for no reason at all. Neither of us have long hair anymore. I suppose you can't imagine me looking like that, can you? We both had long hair and bell bottoms; I wore a suede vest with fringe. Maybe we looked stupid, but back then it was pretty far out, Emily."

She laughed, "When I get off this ship, then that's what I'll wear." Then she stopped laughing, "What's the plan?"

A week later Roderick was driving the new car he purchased to continue his travel across country for his lecture series. But he wasn't alone this time.

"Let's stop somewhere," the girl said. "I gotta get something to eat, and find a ladies room."

"Sure, okay," he said quietly, "the next exit off the highway." And suddenly it came to him that he was on one of the same highways he rode down a century ago with Ralph, their long hair flying in the wind with the windows open, the radio blasting, a guitar in the back of their van. It was as if the road itself was a bridge from the past and into the future, the eternal dark highway that crossed the continent with an endless stream of cars heading nowhere and anywhere.

Finally he pulled over and the car glided slowly into a parking lot. He planned to pull into a dark spot and open the trunk of the car where bottles of blood were kept in a large container, packed in ice. Before she got out he turned to look at her: Hair now jet black, eyes lined with dark makeup, suede jacket with both fringe and brass studs, tight black silk leggings with black leather boots, multiple bracelets and long dangling earrings. She held onto a rolled up magazine. Since dusk she had been flipping through the magazine that she had picked up earlier, but now it was darker and getting harder for her to read it.

"We're in this magazine, you know."

"What?"

"Roderick Moroy, the famous vampire rights activist, and his new significant other. That's what it says. Someone got our picture walking out from a lecture hall, I guess. You're famous, but no one knows who the hell I am, which is good."

He thought a moment, "You know, someday, someone is going to ask who you are. Have you decided about that yet?"

"I'm from Northern California, my parents are descended from people who were hippies a hundred years ago, hippies who left society to live off the land and be one with nature, so I haven't seen much of the big world, because I grew up on our small farm in the middle of the

84

forest. I want to be a fashion designer someday, and an activist, too!"

He smiled slightly, "Have you decided what your name is?"

"Strawberry Fields," she said, "After that real old song you were playing in the car last night when we headed down the highway. I think it kind of sounds like a girl's name, doesn't it?"

"I suppose it does. And most people today won't remember that song anyway."

He watched as she opened the door and got out of the car. They had saved each other's lives, and now he was going to show her the world.

The Children

Six-year-old Stacey was screaming again. Another nightmare.

"Momeeeeee! The gray people are here again! Don't let them take me!"

Tina shuffled out of bed and turned on the light. Another interrupted night's sleep, damn it. She needed to get up at six a.m. for work and didn't need her daughter howling from yet another insane nightmare at two a.m.

"Stacey!" She opened the door to the little girl's bedroom. "There are no gray people. It's a bad dream. Remember what Doctor Peters said? It's just a dream! Okay, sweetie? It's only a dream. Now go to sleep, please, Stacey."

"No, Mommy! No. They were here. The gray people! They say I belong with them. They say I'm really one of them!"

"Stacey, sweetheart. I thought you said the gray people don't talk?"

"They say things with their thoughts, Mommy. They think things, and I can hear what they say, in my head."

"Oh . . . my . . . God."

"Mommy. Please don't be mad."

"I'm not mad, baby. I . . . I just don't know what to do," Tina sobbed. She stopped crying; she needed to be strong for Stacey.

"They want me to go with them, and be with all the other children that belong to them."

At the last session she told Doctor Peters that Stacey seemed normal otherwise, when she wasn't being afraid of the gray people with the big dark eyes that came in the night for her. She played well with others, she liked to color and play dolls, just like other little girls. It was just when she began to rave about the gray people. "Where does all this come from, Doctor?" she asked the child psychiatrist.

He looked at her blankly. "I don't know. I've never seen a case like this before. A lot of children have monsters under the bed. But I've never heard about gray people that come from the sky."

She did not know who Stacey's father was. It was as if she just simply didn't remember who, or what, happened, or where. "I don't know, Doctor. There's like . . . I don't know. Nine months before she was born, there was like an entire day and a half I can't remember about. It's like I have missing time, somehow. I swear, I don't do drugs. And I don't drink. Well, not much. I just don't know. I have no recollection, no memory, of how she came to be." Other than that, she's a completely normal little girl, Tina continued to insist. "She's so smart. She's reading and doing math way ahead of the other kids."

Saturday she thought it would be a good idea to take Stacey to the park. The fresh air would make her forget all the bad dreams, she hoped. And she would get to see other children. Normal children that would just play and not talk about gray people. It was a sunny day, and she could sit on a bench and read a book while Stacey played on the swing set.

Then there was that odd kid hanging around again, about age eleven, but who looked extremely streetwise and never had any parents around. Piper, that was her name, she remembered. She looked thin and underfed, pale, with albino hair. And Tina worried about Piper, that she could be a bad influence on Stacey. Piper seemed to like Stacey and she talked to her, and Stacey was happy when she was around.

She decided to find out more about Piper.

"Piper, sweetie, where are your parents?"

"I do not have parents, Tina," she replied in an odd monotone.

Tina was slightly stunned to be called by her first name by a child, but Piper also seemed to be eleven going on thirty-one. And there was the way she spoke, saying do not rather than don't. What was it with this kid? And she didn't seem to play much, either. She would just hang around, watching the other children play.

"Piper, you must have parents, honey. They must be somewhere. Everyone has parents, right?"

"No."

"Well, isn't that where everyone comes from?"

Piper didn't answer.

"Piper, you do have a home, don't you?" Piper didn't look homeless. Although she was very thin and unhealthy looking, her clothes were clean and appeared new.

"Home?" Piper looked confused.

"Where you go, where you sleep, where you eat. You know, home, Piper."

"I have a home, Tina."

Sheesh, she thought, *this kid is even weirder than my kid!*

Saturday night. Finally Tina could have a small amount of time to herself. She put her daughter to bed and flopped on the worn out couch with a hot cocoa to watch TV. She watched something mindless to keep her from thinking about her problems with Stacey.

"Mommy?"

She looked around. There was Stacey in her pink pajamas and bunny slippers, "Stacey, sweetie, it's late. Why aren't you in bed? Did you have another bad dream?"

"Piper wants me to go to the park to play with the other kids that came down from the sky."

"What? Okay. Now enough of this crazy stuff, damn it, Stacey. I don't want to hear anything more about people that came from the sky! You go to bed. Right now!"

The little girl ran back to her room. She wondered if she was too hard on her. And she wondered if she would ever grow out of it, or end up a permanent resident in a facility somewhere. The thought of her child being locked away made her want to throw up. She grabbed the pillow that was on the couch and buried her face in it so Stacey wouldn't hear her cry.

Hours later she went to Stacey's room to check on her, make sure she was finally quiet and asleep. . . .

She was gone.

"Stacey? Oh my God. Stacey!"

She must have gone to the park, alone, by herself, looking for Piper. She ran to get her purse and find her car keys.

Strangely, the lights around the park that normally were on only at dusk were still on well past midnight. With the lights on, she could see there was actually a group of children there, playing on the swing set, all around Stacey's age. And there she was. Stacey was watching another little girl go up the ladder on the slide.

She parked her car and got out, "Stacey? Stacey, honey? Come over here."

"Mommy! They want me to teach them how to play."

"What?"

"They don't know how to play, Mommy."

"Stacey. Honey. Where are the parents of these kids? Why are they out here, at three in the morning? And you got to answer me."

"They don't have any parents. They came from up there." She pointed.

"What the—?" Tina looked up. And then she saw it. *"Holy sh—!"* She stepped back, "What . . . where did that come from?"

A large, glowing, disc shaped craft hovered silently above. Tina stood motionless, looking up at the space ship.

"It is true, Tina. They do not know how to play." It was Piper. She appeared, as if out of nowhere. "They do not know how to play with toys, or play with puppies or play with kittens, or how to paint or draw or color, or do the things children usually know how to do."

"What the hell is going on, Piper?"

"And they do not have names, or parents, and they do not know what love is. We hope they can learn. When I was much younger, like them, I was given books. I chose my name, after a story in a book, the Pied Piper. That was fifty-three of your years ago. But something was not right when they made me. I did not grow to be tall, like you. Stacey is lucky to have already learned what Earth children already know. And she is more . . ." she paused, "more . . . human."

"Piper? What is going on, really? *And where the hell are you from?"*

"We are not from this Earth. Our planet is dying. The star it orbits has grown dark and cold. We must find a new home. We do not look like you, so we need to collect what you call," she paused again, as if trying to find the right word, "what you call DNA, to become like you, to be able to breathe your air. To exist here. Eventually we will move into your society, interbreed with your species, and your people will know nothing of our existence. Our DNA will mix with that of your people, and soon we will look like you enough to live unnoticed. We will live here, in homes like your homes. We have already replaced some of your leaders. We will get jobs, and have families, like yours. Your planet will then become ours. There will be a new world order."

"What? You . . . you can't do that!"

"We can. And we will."

"It's wrong, Piper. Don't you understand?" She stared at the ship hovering above. "It's just wrong! *Do you people even understand what wrong is?"*

"Wrong? No, Tina. It is not wrong. Your people have nearly destroyed the ecosystem of this world. The air is no longer pure. The water is tainted with the wastes of your civilization. Sludge fills your oceans. The other intelligent life that inhabits the oceans tell us of their sufferings. When we take over, we will rectify all this. We will clean the waters. We will filter the air. We will rebuild the forests that you have burned. The Earth itself cries out to be rid of your people, for Earth itself is dying. We will take this planet. And end all wars. There will no longer be hunger. Or disease. Look, see," Piper gestured toward the playground. "It is already happening. Can you tell if these children of Earth are much different than any other children of Earth?"

She looked at the children on the swing set, gliding back and forth, not laughing, but appearing to enjoy learning how to play. And there was Stacey, standing next to the sandbox, giving instructions to another alien child, "Don't just sit there. You're supposed to, like, make castles, and stuff. Look, I'll show you. You scoop up the sand . . ."

Tina then noticed a small, frail looking child sitting motionless on the swing, staring back at her, as if not knowing what to do.

"I'll help you, sweetie." Tina went to the motionless child, "Look, you hold onto the chains, put your hands on the chains, like this." She took the little girl's hands and placed them, "Like this. Now I'm going to push you. Don't be scared. It's fun. All the other kids play like this." She pushed the child gently, "And when you're all finally here, and we're all finally gone, maybe you'll bring your own children to the park someday, and you can take them to the playground, and teach them how to play. Maybe I'll be here. Maybe not. I'm not sure how I'll fit in with their plans, sweetie, but there's not much I can do about it now. We didn't take good care of this place we call Earth, so now we're going lose it. Maybe we even deserve to lose it? And no one will believe me if I try to warn people, because I didn't believe Stacey. I didn't believe, so it's as much my fault as everyone else's on this planet, isn't it? I guess soon we'll all just be extinct. And there's not much any of us can do about it. *Is there?*"

Vultures

She had a normal life once. Once, long ago, she was a real person. Or she felt like a real person. Now—now she was nothing. And she waited for the inevitable, along with all the other nothing people.

She looked around and could not fathom the vast crowd that surrounded her. All kinds of nothing people: the kinds of people that society just didn't want. Most were homeless, like herself, or probably just poor or lower income. Some just weren't healthy or fit enough to work. Many were children. She could still hear a child whimper off in a distance.

She lost her own child, a little girl, taken away from her when she lost her home; and taken away to where, she did not know. She had a home once, with her daughter, and a job, and a normal life.

But that was before They came.

No one knew where They came from. Some say from outer space. Some say from below the Earth's surface, maybe from Hell. Or from another dimension. Or They were created by evil scientists in a lab and had escaped from somewhere. People around her had all these theories of where the monsters came from.

They were dark grey with horrible wings, long necks and sharp claws. They looked like vultures. Giant vultures. Giant vultures from a nightmare, or from somewhere, not of this Earth.

She had a normal life once, she remembered again; but that was before she lost her job that she had for ten years. She lost her home, and most of her possessions, except for her old but still functional Chevy Impala. It was one of the few things she owned that was paid for, and big enough to sleep in. In the winter, she wrapped herself up in the blankets that she kept from the normal home she once had.

In the parking lot behind the shopping mall, she got to know other people like herself, living out of cars and vans, or sleeping behind recycling bins. They taught her to go into the mall to get warm, to find half eaten donuts or sandwiches in trash bins, to clean up in the public restrooms, and not to ask any of the shoppers for any help, or the police would come down hard on all of them. She and the other people like her lived side by side, unnoticed, next to the people with normal lives.

This went on for about a year.

Once while searching the bins for food she found a newspaper. There was a picture of one of these beings. No one knew what it was, or where it was from, or how many there were. She showed it to the others, the people of the parking lot. One of the men said that he had seen one fly overhead, but he didn't tell anyone, because people would think he was losing it.

From then on, she looked at every thrown away newspaper she could find, and brought them back to show. No one that lived in the parking lot knew what to make of things. One of them decided to clean himself up so he could go into the store that sold expensive TV sets and see if he could get some news.

He came back: No one knew where They were from, but They had met with world leaders, and claimed ownership of the whole planet Earth. The news reporters would say nothing much after that.

Then the round ups started.

Sick people, people who had been out of work too long, people who were in jail or who had been in jail, anyone who was different, any excuse.

And most of all, the homeless.

The people were put in trucks and brought to camps.

And that's where she was now.

She sat on the cold ground, looking up at the normal blue sky, wishing for her normal life back again, and wishing for at least her Chevy to keep warm in. She slept in a barracks at night, with other women. It was always cold.

Then she remembered her history classes from school when she was a kid. These things had happened before, to other people. But now it was happening to her, in Indiana. A camp, sealed off behind a high concrete wall, topped with barbed wire, and men with guns and fierce dogs patrolling the fence.

A short distance away, she heard the voice of a preacher calling out. She looked around and saw him standing on a box.

"They live off greed! Greed, brothers and sisters! They eat at the hearts of all goodness. They devour innocence, and destroy all that is good! It is the work of evil, brothers and sisters! They have always been here, below the surface, controlling the way of things, whispering into the darkened hearts of our leaders, and finally now the gates of Hell have opened from one of the many foul sinkholes that have gutted our cities from all the fracking and global warming, and now finally They come up from Hell to make Themselves known! They have been behind everything, brothers and sisters! They have been behind all wars, the cause of all famine, poverty, and inequality! The filth that is on television. The rotten food that we eat! Pollution! They cause all of it! They have stolen the hearts of humanity and poisoned our thoughts with lust for riches, and make us steal resources from God's precious Earth! The future of our children—"

One of the guards came with his rifle and put an end to it.

She half wondered if what the preacher said were true. Or if he simply had lost it.

The guards. She had been there only a short time but life in the streets had taught her to watch out, and she quickly learned to watch the guards. When there were groups of guards marching about with their rifles, looking important, like they were on a mission, she needed to try to stay out of the way, to live, maybe, for just one more day.

She quickly learned what it was all about.

People would be herded at random and marched into the big building that was at the edge of the camp. It didn't take long for the inmates to figure out what resided in the building, either. For before the guards went on their routine march through the crowds, there would be heard a great shriek, like the shriek of a bird of prey.

Whatever was in the building was hungry, and wanted to be fed. Now. Luckily, again, she managed to avoid the rounding up. She watched from a distance: men, women, children. Many were old. One was in a wheelchair; another shuffled with a limp. And another was disfigured. They took those that were imperfect, or weak somehow, or simply just not beautiful enough.

She wondered how much longer she would last.

97

Sitting on the ground, she looked up at the blue sky, tried to remember her normal life, and felt herself drift off to sleep, probably because she had not slept since her arrival. She fell asleep even on the cold ground.

She slowly awakened, warm in her own bed. Soon the alarm clock would buzz, and she would have to drag herself out of bed and drop her daughter off at daycare and then be off to her boring job. "Mommy?" she heard a delicate voice whisper, "Mommy? Are you coming soon? I'm waiting for you. Over hear, on the other side, Mommy."

"I'm coming," she mumbled. "God. What a crazy bad dream that was." She struggled to sit up and noticed how cold she felt. She shivered. And blinked.

"W-what?"

Suddenly she felt the end of a rifle shoved into her back.

"You. Get up. Now."

She knew it was inevitable.

She got up, and got in line.

She had a normal life once. Once, long ago, she was a real person. A person whose life mattered, a person with a home and a job and who ate three times a day and . . .

"Hurry up!" the guard snarled, "Don't make those hungry wretches wait. You think I like putting up with you people? You people are a drag on this society, that's why you're all here instead of hard working people like me!" And he gave her a hard shove to move her along.

She had a normal life once. She closed her eyes and remembered, as she made her way slowly toward the building, trying to tune out the sound of the screams that came from within.

I Knew There Was Something Weird About This Town!

I always thought there was something weird about this town. I would say to myself, "is it my imagination, or does this town have more than its share of nuts?" But yeah, I found out for sure, something really weird was going on.

Yeah. Really.

Realizing that it wasn't just my imagination started the day I saw the black helicopters fly overhead. At first, there were just a few. Once in a while, I would see them. And then, more recently, there were a lot more of them around. Military type helicopters, I think. Not that I'm an expert on anything military. But the other day I saw them, four freaking black helicopters, flying over the shopping center while I was coming out of the grocery store. And they were in formation, too. I was like, well, that's strange. What's up with that?

But that's not what's really strange about this town. No. Not just the black helicopters. It's the people.

The ones who label me a communist because I don't tend to think exactly like everyone else does. Communist is a rather strong word. I don't think I'm really a communist. It's more like I don't think that the U.S. should start a new war every week, and that instead of starting wars, the government should maybe help the poor rather than be going around blowing stuff up. That maybe finding clean energy would be good thing, instead of killing more people to get more oil. Not that I'm against oil. My old car loves oil, and I love my old car. But there has to be a better way to get oil, rather than blowing up everything and everywhere back to the freaking Stone Age.

Another reason I tend to not fit in this town is because I read. Yeah. I read actual books. They watch TV and listen to talk radio. And I went to college. Not something you would want to admit to in this town, either. Going to college definitely makes you a communist, I guess. In fact, I was told that, to my face, that college brainwashes young people, and teaches young people communism. I was never taught to be a communist in college. Oh, yeah, we talked about socialism in economics class a few times, but that was it. We were never taught to become actual card carrying member communists.

Of course, I stood silent and said nothing when I heard that, not admitting to having an education. In this town, an education is not really a good thing. No. Don't think for yourself, whatever you do. Don't dare disagree. Don't say what you really feel. It's not a good idea. Could get your tires slashed. Or make your reputation worse than it already is. And if you do think for yourself, don't say so in public.

It is kind of odd to have people in this day and age still searching for communists amongst themselves. But the town does have sort of a 1950's feel to it. Even though the cars and a lot of the buildings are new, the attitudes are way out of date. I get funny looks when I say I'd rather work at a job and support myself, than marry and have eight hundred and forty-nine babies and stay home. A lot of the women still have outdated hair, too, using five gallons of hairspray to keep it that way. Who said that college makes you into a communist? A lady with big 60's hair. Yeah, that's right. Time for time warp!

And the men, well . . . some of them just live in a haze of rage all the time, angry at liberals, angry at this minority and that minority, angry at women who won't do what they're told, and angry at people who won't think the way they are supposed to think . . . and just plain angry that things just aren't "the way things should be." You can identify them by the glazed over look in their eyes.

So, yeah, I don't fit in too well around here. In fact, everyone thinks I'm an idiot. Because I read books and see things differently and refuse to listen to the radio stations they listen to. I just don't "think right," if you know what I mean. I'm sure people whisper about me. Yeah, I'm sure they do. "I think she might be a communist!" "Oh, isn't that awful! A godless communist! In our town?" "Yes, and that's not all. I heard she even went to college! And don't repeat this, but they say she reads books!"

It's always been this way, since I can remember. I sometimes wondered if something was in the water, making people crazy. But then I said to myself, "Naw, it can't be. Maybe it's me? Maybe I just don't fit in? Maybe they're right. Maybe I really am an idiot?"

Then came the black helicopters.

And the water smells funny lately sometimes, too, like chemicals. Or was I imagining that, too? And then there were the sudden rages people had, the verbal outbursts, raving against liberals and feminists and this group of people and that group of people, raving against people with foreign accents in general. The road rages on Main

Street, people getting out of their cars to slug each other. And there were the people on Main Street without cars, wandering alone up and down the road, talking to themselves, drifting slowing here and there, going nowhere in particular. All pretty strange for a decent appearing suburb.

Oh, sure there are normal people too. People who don't wander around or rave madly about politics or this or that. *But why does this town have so many whack jobs?*

The day the helicopters flew overhead in formation, that's when I found out.

I thought it was odd they were headed in the direction of my house. I laughed about it. Why would they come to my house? I'm nobody, especially in this town. In fact, I'm less than nobody.

But then late at night, while drifting off to sleep on the couch with one of my useless books, that's when there was a knock on my front door. *"What? Who the hell is that?"*

It was the Men in Black. Oh yeah. Actual Men in Black, as in the See-Eye-Freaking-Aye! There were three of them. Black suits, ties, hats, sunglasses, the whole complete MIB wardrobe. They were like a fashion show for secret agents.

Next thing I knew, I was being thrown in the back of a white van. "Hey. What the hell are you guys doing? I didn't do anything."

"That's what we're going to find out."

When the van stopped they let me out into what looked like a concrete bunker of some kind. I knew it must have been underground because of the coldness and darkness of the place. It was not completely dark. It was lit by small ineffective electric lights suspended from the ceiling. And it was in the same crazy town, because the van did not go far.

"What the hell is this place?"

"We'll ask the questions, not you!"

They walked me down a long dark corridor. I saw military men in fatigues on the way down, men with assault rifles standing around guarding this door or that door. Next I saw a lady in black working a big computer. She was dressed the same except for wearing a skirt instead of pants. The hat just didn't go well with the rest of her secret agent outfit. Finally we went into an interrogation room. Oh yeah, just like on TV. I sat down at a metal table. Two of the MIB's stood by the door, and the other one, apparently the leader, stood by where I sat and began to ask questions.

"Why are you here?" said the MIB.

"Well, you guys brought me here. Why don't you tell me?"

"No. Not that. I mean, why are you in this town?"

"Oh. Well, I was brought up here, and my family lives in this town, so, that's why. It's my hometown."

One of the MIB's by the door said, "Sir, our research indicates she is telling the truth. Our computer searches show that she has lived here all her life."

"Yeah, see," I said. "Now, you tell me, why am I here? Why did you bring me to this military basement? I would like to know? And why are there black helicopters flying over the town? And by the way, why does the drinking water smell funny?"

He pulled out a chair and sat down across from me, "You seem to see things differently than other residents of this town. In a few cases, our experiment has failed. A few people in town, yourself included, still unfortunately manage to be able to think."

"Think?"

"Yes," he sighed, "Think. This town was chosen decades ago for experimentation. The experiment has mostly been proven a great success. The goal was to create a citizenry that would believe what we wanted them to believe, vote the way we wanted them to vote, give to the correct political causes, and so on, so that we may eventually use these mind control techniques throughout the rest of the United States, in order to allow the military industrial complex to continue to exist, unchallenged by peace activists and environmentalists. This town is just one location where we have conducted this type of study. However, in each case, there are always a few people who continue to think for themselves, and we are trying to find out where we have failed with people like you. People who continue to think freely, that is."

"Oh, well, how do you know how I think, after all, I'm not really outspoken. You don't see me walking around carrying signs or anything."

"After reading a few of your emails to some of your friends who live outside of this town, we've figured the experiment didn't work too well on you."

"What? You guys are reading my emails?"

"Not us, specifically. But other people we work with. Secret elements within the government read everyone's emails. Don't take it personally. Everyone's emails and phone calls are being read and listened to, twenty-four seven. So don't worry about it. Your messages indicate that you feel the government should help feed the poor, provide housing for the homeless, find cleaner energy, end wars, and provide better schools. Is that not correct?"

"Well, yeah? So what? What's so bad about that?"

"And you have noticed your neighbors disagree with you to the point of labeling you a communist?"

"Yeah? Is this what this is about? I've never joined to Communist Party, ever. I read one of their brochures once, but that was it. Really."

"No. We don't care if you are or are not, or ever have been, a communist. We want to know why you think for yourself. The people we work for invented the communist scare in the first place to get people to vote for the right politicians, to keep the military industrial complex running. We've been doing it for decades, and it's worked pretty well. Occasionally, we have to find new enemies for the American people to worry about. Communists aren't that popular these days. First we used communists, then we used hippies, then we used liberals in general. Now terrorists are in fashion. Of course terrorism is real. We just put it out in the media more than is necessary to keep it on people's minds all the time so they'll stay worried and frightened and be in favor of war to keep us all in business."

"Oh. I see it works pretty well, then, I guess. You guys in the military industrial complex have a good racket going. But what has it got to do with this town? And why am I here? I have a cat at home who needs me."

"Well, we've got the right combination of chemicals in the water nearly perfected, and the right radio broadcasts for the people to listen to keep their altered minds focused on the things we want them to stay frightened of, but somehow, still, a few people remain untouched by our experimentation. Why? And why you?"

"You mean there are other people in town, like me, who think for themselves?"

"Not many, but a few, such as that eccentric artist fellow on Forest Street who lives in the old restored Victorian with his, err . . . his . . ."

"Boyfriend. Yeah. That's Herb."

"And the older lady who lives by the swamp with the multiple cats and dogs, who always has a sign on her lawn each time there is an election supporting politicians our program doesn't usually endorse."

"Oh, that's Betsy. I guess those people are going to be down in this basement next, huh?"

"When we're done interviewing you, yes. Now, tell us. Why do you think for yourself?"

"I don't know. I guess I just don't fit in with this little small-minded town. I've always been that way. But you guys don't need to worry. It's not like I'm going to infect the population with my thinking, because no one listens to me, and people think I'm an idiot anyway. I'm just someone they all whisper about and talk about and stare at. It's not easy, you know, being able to think for yourself in this town. Everyone else being high on the chemicals in the water, and listening to the talk radio you broadcast around here. It's just not easy being one of the few people who can think. It's like being surrounded by zombies, except they don't want to eat my brain, because you've already eaten theirs for them."

"Now, we must ask you, do you drink the water at all? From the faucet in your home?"

"Well, yes, I did, until it began to smell really bad. Then I bought bottled water. A lot of people in town say bottled water is for dumb college educated liberals, so what does that tell you? Are these chemicals in the water recently? Or have they always been there?"

"The chemicals have always been in the water system of your town, we've just increased the amounts, this being an election year. How about other aspects of your lifestyle? You say you don't listen to talk radio?"

"No. I don't watch much TV, either. I like to read."

"Read? Oh, that's bad. Reading is very bad for our program. Taking in knowledge by way of reading affects the brainwaves, so it makes it more difficult to control people. There." He looked at the other two Men In Black. "Gentlemen. We have our answer. She reads books. It makes her able to think."

The other two looked at each other and nodded.

"Well, what are you going to do now?"

"Simple. Make a few phone calls, cut funding to the library, and cut funding to the school."

"I can still go out of town to find a bookstore, you know."

"Oh, that's fine. It's too late for you. You already know how to think. We have to keep books away from the rest of the people in town. Just keep them listening to raving lunatics on talk radio and watching violence on television, and they'll all be fine."

"Okay. Well, you're not going to shoot me now, are you?"

"No. We don't need to. No one listens to you, anyway. Who would believe you when you warn everyone in town that the CIA is putting drugs in their drinking water, and putting subliminal messages in their radio and on their TV shows? They already just laugh at you, so why would you bother to warn those people?"

"You're right. No one listens to me, anyway."

"We're just going to drive you home and continue on with the rest of our plans."

"Oh. Okay. Well, it's been interesting, but I'd like to go home right now."

"Fine," he called to the other Men In Black, "You can take her back home to her cat."

He shook my hand, *"Thank you for your time, miss. Now we know what the next step of our experiment must be."*

(This story is for entertainment only. The author intends no political message.)

The Wolf at Your Door

I arrived at work one morning when a co-worker was in a state of near hysteria telling her strange story, "And then I saw it, there it was at the edge of the woods, just staring at me! It was a wolf! And I ran so fast! I just know it wasn't a dog."

A wolf. In the suburbs. Very hard to believe. Wolves do not live in suburbs, nor are they supposed to move into upscale neighborhoods. This is the stuff that ghost stories are made of.

And all of a sudden, all kinds of creatures are roaming around through the 'burbs, including but not limited to, wolves, or more likely, coyotes and wolf-coyote hybrids. In my location, we hear odd tales of not just wolves, but mountain lions, moose, black bears, and bobcats, casually wandering down Main Street as if they belong there.

Stranger things have happened. In Great Britain, where there is practically no wilderness left, there is the notorious Fortean legend of the "Black Dog." The old tale goes that mysterious black dogs, or black wolves, materialize at dark crossroads, baying in terrible, wretched despair, appearing before disaster strikes, as if to send a message from the other side.

This tale was especially popular during the Victorian Age, and Sir Arthur Conan Doyle's tale *The Hound of the Baskervilles* is said to have been inspired by the legend of this "spectral hound."

Although unprovoked wolf attacks on humans are rare, modern people still hold on to a superstitious dread of the wilderness. But the wolf, as well as many other wild creatures, seems to also fascinate us. As many times as we listen to terrifying fairy tales such as Little Red Riding Hood, we can never forget the heroic she-wolf who rescued Romulus and Remus. Jack London's stories of wolves seem more about noble savages than savage predators. We tell ourselves that we hate them and fear them, yet they also fascinate us. Why?

And why are they, and other wild creatures, now materializing all around us, invading suburbs, and even populated cities, turning busy streets and backyards into wilderness? Suburban areas are now populated by the coyote, considered by many to be just a "small wolf." There have been alleged sightings of wolves, and also mountain lions and lynx roaming mysteriously through even the so-called upscale neighborhoods. In some cities, shrieking raptors fill the skies—hawks and even eagles have been seen flying over tall buildings.

I remember that in the late 70's, in a rough blue collar town in my home state of Massachusetts, there were several odd stray mongrel dogs existing in the local stinking dump. These poor, pitiful, lost creatures made their lives in abandoned trucks and ate off society's trash, yet they caused a tremendous panic for a few ridiculous years. People angrily wrote to local papers that they were concerned about their children's safety, they were worried about the savage packs of "wolves and dogs" running wildly throughout the dump. It didn't really matter that most kids stayed out of the smelly dump and that no one lived for miles around the wretched place. The people demanded that local authorities march in and shoot these crazed killer beasts! I do not recall one report of anyone being bitten, however, one man wrote to the local paper and claimed that he was "chased."

Like a UFO sighting, a single wild animal sighting often results in a rash of very excited phone calls to police and local news stations. A coyote! No, it was a wolf! Not a wolf, but an entire savage pack! But then someone else sees a puma, which someone else claims is really a lioness, maybe it escaped from the circus. It doesn't matter that the circus hasn't been in town for twenty years. Every little cocker spaniel becomes a cause for extreme panic.

And we love it, don't we?

Why? Because we need them, that's why.

What else would we do with our miserable little lives? We wake up, get ready for work, drive to work in a small air conditioned vehicle, go into a climate controlled building, and sit in front of a computer all day, then we go home and eat our frozen dinners. And if we are lucky we can see a "nature show" on TV. Or we might watch a televised version of "White Fang." Then while trying to sleep we hear a stray dog bay at the moon . . . *Or was it a wolf?*

There is no doubt about it, wildlife is invading the suburbs, either in physical or spectral form. Could these creatures really be apparitions? Could they be the Spirit Animals of Native American legend, come to us to bring messages from the Great Spirit of the Forest? Are they here to save us, to invite us back into the natural world, to tell us that All Is Forgiven, and that we can come home now?

In the daylight, we tell ourselves that they don't belong here, they belong in some strange mysterious place we refer to as "way out in the woods." But if we turn out the lights, open a window, let the fresh night air in, and listen to the sounds of the distant night forest, then can we hear them calling us? Calling out for us to come back? If we listen for the wailing voice of the wilderness, what will it tell us, about ourselves, and about what we as civilized and domesticated people have sadly lost?

The Native Americans honored Wolf and his little brother Coyote. They were hunters, fellow warriors, messengers of the Great Spirit. I sometimes hear him, far away, calling out from a distant hillside, right before dawn. One night I saw him, running up my driveway when I came home after working three hours overtime. Was he trying to tell me to run away with him? Leave the computers, and the paperwork, and the desk, and come away with me to be Wild and Free?

Or was he just out looking for trash?

As we become more bored and boring, more tied down by our machines, more and more wild things start to manifest themselves. They run down major highways, dashing in front of our SUV's on dark roads, roaming through our professionally kept and well-manicured suburban backyards. When we go jogging to reclaim our lost youthful figures, are we really running with the wolves? Are they trying to tell us something, to remind us of who we really are and where we really belong?

They cry out from the wilderness, and we must listen.

Not In My Backyard!

Marcus heard a rustle in the bushes by the driveway as he got out of his jet black BMW, and then heard a familiar snarl. He reached into the car for his briefcase, and then he looked around to see the glowing eyes reflected in the headlights.

"What's up, Penelope?" He used her full name to annoy her, instead of calling her Penny.

The slate gray she-wolf stared silently at him a moment, then she stood up to attain the form of a woman, "I'll tell you what's up, Marc. Trouble, that's what. You should have been at the town meeting."

"Oh what is it now, Penny? There's not enough in the budget to fill the multitude of pot holes on your avenue?"

"Don't be a jerk, Marc. This is serious. They're going to sell the woods to developers."

He slammed the car door. "Huh? What did you just say?"

"You heard me. I'm calling a meeting at the usual place. Be there, for once, will yah? Sometimes I think you care more about that BMW than you do the rest of the Pack." She went back down on all fours, and in an instant was covered in fur. She melted back into the forest.

He followed the long drawn out wail of wolf song as he made his way into the forest to meet with the others. He jumped over a mud puddle, so as to not soil his white paws. He did not want to go to this meeting. He had another meeting to be at first thing in the morning with the Board of Directors of his company to discuss the coming staff layoffs and he wanted to at least appear to be awake. Couldn't this wait until the next full moon? He didn't like it. And he didn't like Penelope. He still felt he should have been elected pack leader. He was stronger, he could hunt better, and he had an MBA. But no, they chose her.

Finally he arrived at the clearing in the middle of the forest. Penelope was standing on a boulder, in human form, in her usual jeans and sneakers, addressing the assembled Pack.

"There will be fifty luxury condominium units, and a golf course with a clubhouse. There is also talk of the possibility of a strip mall."

Someone snarled. Another barked. And then a whimper.

"Yes, that's right. A strip mall. Can you all imagine it? A liquor store, a nail salon, a convenience store, right at the edge of our hunting ground. And here will be the golf course, right where we are now."

Peter stood up and became human so he could talk, "That really, really sucks, Miss Roberts!"

Marcus was amused. It seemed like the kid was just a cub yesterday, and today he was trying to decide which college he would go to, and he still called Penelope Miss Roberts.

"That's right, Pete, it does really suck," she said.

He sat on the moss-covered ground and yawned; and then scratched his ear with his hind foot. Then, horrified, he realized the possibility he may have a flea. He had never had a flea before. What was the world coming to? Just yesterday he paid $500 to have his BMW professionally polished, and today a flock of birds made a mess of it. And now . . . he had a flea. It was all most unpleasant. And now he had to sit and listen to Penelope. Well, he said to himself, he didn't like the possibility of the forests being demolished either. There would be no place left to chase rabbits after a hard day looking at spreadsheets. Besides, it could drive property values down. Yes, it was all very unpleasant indeed.

Next Betsy stood up. She transformed slowly, and whimpered as she stood up. She was old, and her arthritis was beginning to trouble her more and more. "Well," she finally spoke, "what are we going to do? We don't own the woods. We wish we did, but we don't, Penelope." Betsy remembered when the forest was given to the town by the estate of Edmund St. George, the eccentric millionaire who owned the paper mill that had closed long ago. The forest was literally given to the town to be a bird sanctuary. "It should be ours, but it isn't. I knew this would happen someday. I just hoped I wouldn't live to see it. You can't fight city hall."

"But we have to fight city hall. We can't all just pack up our belongings and all move somewhere else. Where would we go? Besides, who wants to live in a city? I don't. And I'm sure none of you do, either!"

The others agreed loudly. Those who were human went back to their wolf form. They barked, they bayed; they howled out their sad rage and cried into the dark night.

Marcus awoke at the sound of his alarm clock and rolled over in bed. Six o'clock. He stumbled into the shower, turned it on hot, and still worried about the possible flea.

116

He picked his most expensive suit, grabbed a coffee and knew he'd be exhausted at the meeting. He opened the front door and picked up his newspaper.

"What the—?"

The headlines were the usual uninteresting crap. But the small feature at the lower corner of the front page got his attention. "Are There Wolves in St. George Bird Sanctuary?" People had reported hearing wolves in the forest before, but never so loudly as last night.

"Oh crap. Now they'll shoot us all so they can have their stupid golf course. Thanks, Penelope!" He threw the paper in the trash and left.

He had a lousy day at work. The Board of Directors wanted to postpone the layoffs. It was that damn bleeding heart Smithers. "The jerk should have been a social worker," he snarled to himself as drove off the highway exit towards home. He wouldn't shut up all during the meeting about "They have to feed their families." He said, "Smithers, the corporation doesn't make profit by feeding families, we make a profit by doing business." He knew what he'd like to do with that Smithers. He'd like to rip out his throat, that's what he'd like to do, but he didn't like getting himself all blood splattered. It would stain his perfect fur.

The BMW rounded the corner towards the forest as he wondered to himself, "Will this be one of the last times I see these familiar old trees?" He wasn't even sure if he cared anymore. He remembered one day Penelope said he was getting too civilized. He snarled back something about the business world being a jungle full of savage beasts.

117

And then he saw the crowd of people standing at the gateway to the bird sanctuary. Some carried signs. There was a TV news van. He slowed down, and pulled to the side of the road to look.

There were more than a few people. He guessed at least fifty. They chanted, "Save endangered species! Save endangered species! Save endangered species!"

He watched Penelope speaking to the reporter, "Not only will this destroy a beautiful forest, but these condos will take away the habitat of the endangered wolf. I mean, who wants a strip mall in their backyard? I don't want a strip mall in my backyard, and I'm sure the wolves don't, either. If the wolves could talk, I think I know what they would say about the condos going into their forest. They would say it really sucks."

Marcus watched, and laughed quietly to himself. He looked at the crowd and saw some of his fellow werewolves in their human form. There was Peter, in a t-shirt that said "PETA." And old Betsy too, carrying a sign that said, "Save Our Bird Sanctuary." And there were others. There was overweight Brian, the donut eating accountant who couldn't catch a rabbit and got sprayed by a skunk last month. There was Lucy who ran a day care center and liked to chase minivans. There was Brendan. The other wolves thought he might be gay. And Dawn. He liked Dawn. She bit the you-know-what off a rapist last year. The rest of the Pack chased the creep out of town and had fun doing it.

He drove his car up closer and called to Penelope. The reporter finally went to talk to the other protesters. "Hey, Penny. What's up?"

"You can see what's up, Marc."

"You know what? This crazy plan of yours just might work." He looked at her and smiled, "You're okay, Penny. You know that? You're okay." He hit the gas and sped off. Maybe Penelope was a good pack leader after all. He finally agreed with her about something. He didn't want the condos, or the golf course, or the strip mall either.

"Nope. Not in my backyard."

Preacher Wolf

Reverend Billy woke up suddenly, as if startled. He rolled out of bed, looked around, and looked at the clock. He had overslept again. That was bad. He had a lot of work to do, just like he did every day. Passing pamphlets, street preaching, and inviting people to come to the sermons that he held each week at the local trailer park.

He got up, and looked in the mirror. There were strange bloodied stains on his face again. He could not understand why. A message from the Lord? It must be. Reminding him that the precious blood of His Son Jesus Christ was shed each and every day by the evil doings of the liberals and feminists that have taken society away from the moral teachings of the Bible.

And he worked every day to change all that.

He went to his closet to find which suit had the least amount of lint on it. They were all cheap, but some day, when his ministry became more powerful, he would send for an entire wardrobe from Europe. That was strange, he wondered—his best suit had a rip in the shoulder. He knew it was a cheap suit but he expected it to hold up better than that. Oh well. He got something else and got his act together.

While having a fast cup of coffee he looked at the newspaper. Another body found mutilated. It was a homeless man. This was further proof that liberalism and immorality had destroyed American society. Of course the crime rate was going up, he understood, because women were working at jobs outside the home, instead of

120

behaving like submissive wives should behave, and staying home to raise their children with good moral values.

He arrived at the trailer park in his Cadillac and the crowd was already eagerly waiting for him. They loved him, and he knew it. And he loved the adoration from the audience. He stood on the grass while the people sat on the ground and he held the Bible in the air, "Friends. Americans. Christians! It's time to take back this great country of ours, take it away from the liberals and the feminists and the homosexuals!"

"Amen!" They shouted.

"It's time to bring this great country back to Jesus!"

"Praise be to Him!" a man with long gray hair and a stained t-shirt shouted.

"It's time to take America back from the evil, sinful influence of rock and roll music, and to remove from our nation's schools teachers who let our children learn about evolution and other false science, to send women back to their homes where they belong, and to . . ." He went on for an hour, pausing to let the crowd cheer or yell "Amen."

Finally after the sermon he went among the people and answered their Bible questions, talked to them, and counseled them.

A young woman with sad eyes approached him, "Preacher. My husband's been out a work a long time. You think it would be all right if I got me a job?"

"What's your name, child?"

"Becky."

"Becky, my child. God loves you. And that's why He made you for your special ordained place, in the home."

A middle aged man came up to him, "Preacher. My wife and I kinda . . . well, you know . . . our son . . . well, can we talk over here?"

"Err, of course," Reverend Billy wondered what it could be about. They walked away from the crowd a bit.

"Well, Preacher. We . . . sort a think maybe our son might be . . . you know. He might be gay."

"My friend." The expression on his youthful face turned dark and grave. "You and your wife must pray. Pray that his soul might be saved."

It was a good day. He made enough to cover his rent. He planned to spend the rest of the afternoon sitting on the back step in the heat of the Alabama sun with a cold beer. He opened the can and took a sip and wondered about the murder he read about in the paper. More and more bodies were being found in the woods ripped to shreds. Probably the work of Satanists. He smiled. He would lead the holy war when the culprits were found. It would get in the paper, maybe even on the TV. He'd get enough donations to rent space for his church. He would finally have his ministry in an actual building. Not the mega-church he dreamed about. But it would be a start. He admitted to himself, he was ambitious for a Christian.

But it was all for the glory of the Lord.

He went indoors after a few beers and went to watch television. He did not have cable, and there was nothing on but immorality, and game shows. The news was on, but the media was influenced by liberals so he didn't watch it. It was a hot night, and the fan hummed its background noise. One of these days, he promised himself, he'd have air conditioning. And a computer. And a new Cadillac. And closet full of good suits.

Slowly he fell asleep. The TV control fell to the cheap, never vacuumed carpet.

Reverend Billy awakened again in a state of confusion. He found himself not in his own bed, but in the forest. He looked up at the sky. The moon was full, making the night almost as bright as day.

He didn't know how he came to be in the woods. He didn't even know where he was, or how far he was from town. How did he get here? Was it a dream? A sign? A message from the Lord? He did not know. He prayed that God would show him what it all meant.

He looked down at his hands.

They were covered in blood.

"What?"

He looked again. He had no hands. Instead, he had claws.

And they were saturated in warm, fresh blood.

He looked around. There, on the ground before him, was the body of a young woman, ripped to shreds, maimed, her throat torn out.

It must be a vision, he told himself. The Lord is showing me what is happening to our society, what the lack of morality has done.

He would find his way out of the woods, find his way home, and read scripture until the Lord told him what he should do next.

Finally, he made his way out of the forest. He shuffled his way through bushes, through the swamp, through the field that was by the main roadway, and found something he recognized. He finally saw the light—the light from the neon sign that hung in the window of the liquor store that was down the street from the boarding house. He did not like the liquor store and he had unsuccessfully passed a petition to ban the liquor store from town. He didn't have enough signatures. He would try again next year.

It wasn't that he was against alcohol. It was the people that he saw going in the store. Some of them had tattoos; and some of them rode up on motorcycles. Obviously, he knew, they must have very sinful lifestyles.

He walked by the liquor store and up the street that led to the place he rented. There were no lights on in the boarding house, but his Cadillac was in the driveway. Its chrome shined in the moonlight.

He was home.

He opened the door, wandered in, went up the stairs to where his rooms were, and turned the lights on. Fortunately, everyone else in the boarding house was asleep. It wouldn't look good for a Reverend to be out late at night—people might talk.

He decided to go to bed instead of studying scripture. He was tired. He'd get his answers from the Lord in the morning, after breakfast.

He went into the bathroom to soak a cloth in cool water, wash the sweat off his face. But then he looked in the mirror.

There, staring back at him, was a wolf.

He looked down at his hands again, this time in the light. They were claws, and they were covered in dried blood. He looked himself over. His clothes were torn, ripped and covered with mud and leaves.

And then he realized the real truth, that all the murders that had taken place every full moon, the brutal crimes that he had been reading about in the local paper, were not caused by Satanists, or liberals, or homosexuals, or feminists, or any other unholy thing he could think of.

He looked again at himself in the mirror. And finally, he had his answer.

I Tried To Warn Them

I tried to warn them. Really. I did! But they wouldn't listen! I guess they were too cool to listen to someone like me. I mean, if you're not on the cheerleading squad, or the football team, you're like nobody.

Nobody. Like me.

So I guess they wouldn't listen when I told them it might be kind of dangerous to play with that Satanist stuff and go through that old book that they stole and try to raise up some demons from Hell. I guess they thought it would be cool, or something. But I told them that it could be dangerous.

And what did they say? They said, "You're a baby!" and, "She's just jealous because we don't hang out with her!" and, "What's a matter, you scared the creepy crawlies gonna get yah?"

It all started when that old book was stolen from the library. You see, at the library in our town, they have this small room where these really old books are kept in a glass case, and the case is locked. I suppose because the books are so old, maybe people think they're valuable or something. To me, they're just old books. But one of the books was always locked in its own case alone, and people said it was an old magic book that dated back to when they had witch trials. They say the witch hunters found the book. It had always been locked up, so no one probably opened it for a long time, maybe it's been even hundreds of years since it's been read.

Then it was stolen. It was in the newspaper about the old book being stolen, the glass case smashed into, and all that. But no one really seemed to care much about it. Most people thought it was just an old book, except the people who said it was really an old witch's book. I even went to the library myself, to make sure that was the one that was stolen, and I went into the room with the old books. So, yeah, it was the magic book that was missing. It was gone.

That was the only one that they took.

At that time, I didn't know who "they" were. I didn't know who took it. Most people thought it was just stolen because it was old and valuable.

But when I was walking home through the woods, that's when I saw them: A small group of the most obnoxious kids in school. And they had the book. There was cute blonde Chrissie, the head of the cheerleading squad. And Randall, the captain of the football team. I guess Chrissie was just there because of Randall. Chrissie just followed Randall everywhere like a dog and whatever Randall thought was cool, Chrissie thought it was cool, too. Chrissie was pretty, but she just wasn't into thinking too deeply or thinking for herself.

There was Trent. Oh, naturally, Trent. Trent was the one who set fire to this unpopular girl's messy and smelly hair. It was supposed to be funny according to Trent, but she ended up in the hospital. Then Trent told all the grown-ups how she set the fire herself, and no one dared say otherwise, or else they'd be set on fire too. So the poor girl ended up in a mental hospital after being treated for burns, because everyone in charge of the school was telling her parents she set herself on fire, just because Trent said she did it to herself. I don't know why anyone believed a word Trent said. After all, Trent always carried a lighter, and a switchblade. So even though the other kids figured Trent really did set the girl on fire, no one dared talk. Trent had long greasy hair and always wore black.

Then there was Chip, too. I was kind of surprised at Chip. He was for sure headed for Ivy League. Chip was the guy everyone said had a future. It wasn't that Chip was smart. No. He was as dumb as concrete. But his dad was rich, so he had a future and his future included Ivy League, I guess. Everyone else, even if they were real smart, they were headed for community college if they were lucky.

I came into the field beyond the woods where the path would lead up toward where my backyard was. What was I doing there? Heck, on the other side of the woods was the street where the strip mall was, and the comic book store was in the strip mall. Plus also the candy store. That's all. That's one of the reasons why I'm nobody. Because I like comic books. It's okay for a guy to like comic books, but if you're a girl and you like comic books, then you're like weird or something. I don't know why. But that's the way it is.

So anyway, I wasn't in the woods to do drugs or anything. Just cutting through so I didn't have to walk all the way down the main street and then go down the side street toward my house. I just cut through the woods, like a lot of kids did since the comic book store opened up. It was also mainly because someone stole my bike a few weeks before. I still think it was Trent, but I wouldn't say anything about that and get set on fire, or something.

Anyway, I was heading back toward my house and came upon the most mismatched bunch of popular morons from high school I ever saw. Blonde Chrissie in her short skirted cheerleader uniform, giggling at Randall. Trent all in black with a lit up joint, long black hair hiding half his face. And then there was Chip. I never figured these jerks would hang around with each other.

First thing I heard was Chip say, "Gimme some of that joint, Trent."

Trent said, "Get your own."

And what did Chip do? He actually reached into the pocket of his own jacket and pulled out a joint, "Okay. Gimme a light."

Trent went for his lighter and lit Chip's joint.

Then I saw the book, and that's how I knew they were the ones who stole it. Randall was carrying it. He looked through it while he walked through the field following Trent and Chip, "I can't understand a word in this crazy book, Trent. You sure this is a good idea?"

Chrissie looked at the book while Randall held onto it, "What do all those funny words mean, Randy?"

"Dunno. Maybe Trent knows. He's the expert in this stuff. Hey, Trent –

"It's Latin, dummy. Gimme that, will yah," Trent grabbed the book from Randall.

Then Chip saw me, "Hey, look."

I was like, Oh my God, they see me.

"What're you doing here?" giggled Chrissie. "This is our thing. You weren't invited!" Then she saw the comic books rolled up in my hand, "Oh, what a loser. Look, you guys. She still reads those stupid comic books."

"At least I didn't steal them," I said. "What are you doing with that old book?"

"None of your business," said Trent.

"We're Satanists!" giggled Chrissie, as if it were funny.

"So, like, why are you Satanists?" I asked. She looked at me like it was a dumb question. I don't know why anyone would want to be a Satanist. I mean, doesn't that mean you just go to Hell when you die? And who wants to go to Hell? It's stupid to end up in Hell, right? I mean, all you do when you get to Hell is like suffer forever, right? Finally, someone answered the question.

"Because we're cool and you're not," said Chip, puffing his joint.

Trent finished his own joint and smirked, "We're gonna conjure up some demons from Hell. It will be cool. Wanna watch?"

"Isn't that kind of dangerous?" I said.

"You're a baby!" Chrissie said, "She's just jealous because we don't hang out with her!"

Trent flipped through the book until he found a page he liked, "What's a matter, you scared the creepy crawlies gonna get yah?"

"Naw," I lied. I was scared. But not of the devil. I was afraid of these freaks. I mean, okay, so I might be a loser because I read dumb comic books, but these guys were Satanists. They were so stupid they might really do something like that, "I gotta go home, okay?"

"Oh, so you can read your comic books?" snarled Chrissie.

"At least I'm not reading about Satan. Okay? Bye." I started walking again.

"Hey Trent," said Chip, "Let's have a human sacrifice."

I started walking faster now.

"Naw," said Trent. "Someone will find the body, then they'll have cops all over, and people will be asking questions, and people will finally figure out it was me that burnt that dumb girl's hair, and I'll end up in juvenile detention. Come on, you guys, let's forget her and get this thing going. No one listens to her, anyway, even if she does tell. We gotta raise some demons so we can take over the school like we planned, right?"

"The school, nuthin'," said Chip. "Take over the whole town, dude. You think too small, Trent. First the town, then the whole country."

"And maybe the world," giggled Chrissie. Everything that she said came out in giggles. She was so annoying, I don't know why they didn't make her the human sacrifice.

I kept walking faster.

"Oh look," Chrissie giggled again, "She's running away."

Okay, so I was running. I could deal with any one of them, if any one of them was alone. But they were all together. And when idiots like them get together, there's sure to be a lot of trouble.

I kept running towards home, but I could hear them behind me, reciting the words out of the book. It was Trent reading out loud. Then I could smell sulfur. At first, I thought that stupid Trent was burning stuff again, or he dropped a joint and set the field on fire, until I realized that sulfur is supposed to be associated with the devil or something. I began to smell smoke, too. I stopped and turned around when I heard this rumbling sound. I looked and I was totally amazed to see this hole open up in the middle of the field in front of where they all stood, flames coming out of it. I ran faster now. I ran all the way home. I didn't even turn and look when I heard the explosion.

The hole is still out there in the field that's behind the woods. If you walk through the woods and come to the field, you can still see it. People say it's just a sinkhole that opened up all of a sudden. But don't get too close, because it goes all the way to Hell. They are all reported as missing now, all of them. Chrissie, Randall, Trent, and Chip. All of them are missing. People in town say no one knows what happened to them. But I know where they went. They all went to Hell. I guess they didn't know what they were doing with that book. Instead of being able to control the powers of demons, I guess they just opened a gateway to Hell and got dragged into it.

Good riddance.

Chip's dad hired a private detective and put up a big reward if he's ever found, but they'll never find him. Unless Chip's dad ends up in Hell himself, he'll never see his son again. Chrissie's mom is all over the TV and crying her eyes out on camera, saying, "Please! Whoever took my baby! Bring her home!" It's like she's enjoying being on TV. Chrissie is not coming home, lady. The devil took her. Randall's dad got the football team to help search the woods, but they'll never find him. They don't know enough to look down the sinkhole. And I guess Trent is burning in Hell, so now he knows how that girl felt when he ignited her messy hair.

I don't go through the woods much anymore. It's too scary. But sometimes, just sometimes, I walk to the edge of the woods where it opens up to where the field is, and look at the sinkhole. If you stare at it long enough, you can almost see an orange glow. And if you listen hard enough, sometimes you can hear the cries of the damned.

What if You Met the Real Thing?

"Is Shade your first, or last name?" Duffy wondered out loud as he wolfed down his burger. "Like, when the professor calls out names?" He was an overweight young man who wore a jacket and sweatshirt with the logos of his various favorite sports teams.

"Last," he answered simply. The untouched coffee sat in front of him getting cold. He had agreed to come to the cafeteria with the rest of the small group that sat near him in Professor Garabaldi's night class. "First name Wilton." Wilton dressed plainly; new blue jeans, a steel gray cotton cable knit sweater under a brown leather jacket.

"So, like, what do you think of Garabaldi's class?" Ashley asked in an excited voice. She wore a black leather cropped jacket, tight black spandex pants, a spiked black leather dog collar, along with deep red lipstick and dark eyeliner.

"Yeah," mumbled Eddie, who sat next to her. He was casual while she was overly made up, baseball cap on backwards, one gold stud earring, baggy jeans, and high top sneakers, "So, how d'yah like this Medieval folklore thing?"

"Well—" Shade began, and he thought carefully before continuing.

"Like, it was so cool tonight," Ashley interrupted, "This class on vampires. I loved it! I can't wait 'til the next class."

"You are fascinated by that sort of thing?" Shade asked her quietly.

"Yeah. Like, it would be so cool, I mean, to meet a real one!"

Eddie laughed, "Knew you would say that. You're spookier than that crazy professor is!"

"Shut! Up!" She swatted at his hat with her well-manicured hand, displaying multiple silver rings and black nail polish. "What do you think, Wilton?"

He thought a moment, so he could answer carefully, "If his theory was correct, that the legends of vampires are based somehow in reality, and that there are still a few in existence in this century." He hesitated, "well, maybe his ideas about them are all wrong to begin with."

"What d'yah mean, all wrong?" Duffy asked with a mouth full of food.

"Let us say, in theory," although Shade appeared to be as young as the rest of the people at the table, he sounded somehow older, more mature, "if vampires do in fact exist, then why is Professor Garabaldi, and why is everyone in general, so very certain that they are all such terrible monsters?" And he still did not touch his coffee. "What if they just live much like the majority of people?"

"They're all such monsters 'cause they drink blood! Ain't that scary enough for yah, Wilton?" Duffy reached for a handful of fries.

"But Duffy, humans are not the only living creatures that can supply blood. Isn't it logical that any large mammal would suitable? There is a slaughterhouse at the edge of this town, isn't there? So it's a good location for," he stopped. "After all, you eat meat. Are you a terrible monster?"

Duffy didn't answer. Instead he continued to attack everything on his plate.

"Like, yeah, that's right," Ashley said. "I never thought of that."

"This whole entire conversation sounds real weird to me," Eddie sipped his coke and stated that he longed for a cigarette but that he was trying to quit.

"Think of it this way, Ashley," Shade looked directly at her. "If vampires do exist, in this century, then they must work, pay taxes, vote, worry about crime and social disorder, and worry about the economy and the environment, just as must as everyone else does. They could have families, hopes and dreams, like everyone else."

She looked at him. He was good looking, and his face was fair like ivory, and his hair was dark like hers. But he was unfortunately just so normal. She giggled, "But it's the power!" She stressed the word *power*. "That's what's so awesome. The power over others! And I like it that they dress so cool, too!"

"Oh that's right," he sighed, "the legend of some ancient and wise immortal master vampire who controls a vast legion of undead as well as his mortal slaves. Now that is truly precious, isn't it? I know someone who loves that story."

Ashley giggled again and reached into her black leather purse for a stick of gum. She offered it to him. *"But is has to be like that!"*

"No thank you. And it isn't."

"Wilton. If you weren't so damn good looking, you'd be depressing me right now."

"So, hey," Eddie broke his silence. "Why do you take this class anyway?"

"Actually, several months ago, there was an article in the local paper about Professor Garabaldi. It said that he researches vampires, for real. Or so he believes. So then I signed up, to research Garabaldi." Shade leaned back in his chair. The artificial light from the ceiling above reflected in his luminous eyes, "I was curious to meet with him, before he left for Romania."

"So, like, what are you gonna do after the semester?" Ashley seemed to just like talking to him, Shade noticed. And he found it amusing.

"Nothing much. Just go back to all the many other dull things I've been doing."

"You are so damn normal!" she complained.

"So are you, Ashley."

The two boys laughed in unison. Duffy nearly choked on the last of his food, "What? Her? Normal?"

"I am not!" she shot back. And then she laughed too.

"Yes you are, Ashley. You don't know it yet, but you are." He stood up and tossed his Styrofoam coffee cup into the trash. It was full and it splattered as it landed.

Finally Eddie tossed away his half empty cold drink and Duffy got up to put away his tray as well. "Yah know, Wilton," and Duffy pointed directly at him, "you are almost as strange as she is. But you're okay." He turned and walked out of the cafeteria and Eddie followed him. "See yah next class."

He watched as Ashley gathered together her things, her oversized purse, her disorganized notes and textbooks, "Ashley?"

She looked up and smiled, "Yeah?"

"What if you met the real thing?"

"What? I'd be scared to death if I did!" She suddenly looked frightened, then she smiled again. "Besides, it ain't real. It's just that crazy old Garabaldi. He did too much dope in the sixties." And then she left, following the boys into the parking lot.

And finally he did the same. He left the cafeteria and headed into the dark parking lot to his car.

The drive home was uneventful. He pulled up into the driveway and unlocked the front door of the restored Victorian home he shared with a few others, and entered the dimly lit hallway. Mariah came quietly around the corner to greet him as he put his leather jacket away in the closet. She wore her velvet wine colored dress and carried her silver gray tabby cat, "Well? Anything interesting happen tonight?"

He bent to kiss her pale cheek. "Not really. No. Garabaldi leaves the campus right after class and just goes home. I will catch up to him, eventually."

"Calvin wants to see you." She bent to put the cat down.

He sighed. "I'll just tell him the same thing, then," and he proceeded upstairs.

Calvin was sitting at this desk as he usually did late at night, processing other people's taxes and going through their volumes of paperwork so he could advise them how to manage their finances. The radio played softly in the corner of the small dark office. He looked up from his computer screen. "Come in, Wil."

He drifted in slowly and sat down, sinking into a very much worn out leather chair. "What's up, Cal?"

"Any contact with our friend yet?" He took a sip from a mug that was next to the keyboard.

"Not yet. He just lectures very excitedly about legends of the terrifying undead, sounds as if he really takes his stuff seriously, almost always wears the same tweed suit, carries this overstuffed worn out falling apart brief case. Typical full of himself academic. Then he just wanders back home after class. Has no life. Office hours are morning and afternoon. But, I did find out where he usually parks. I was thinking of catching up with him as he goes to his car."

"There's an idea," Calvin agreed. "Then you can meet with him, help him correct his so called research project."

"I'll need to catch up with him before he leaves for Eastern Europe. He expects to find something of importance, discover his obsession in either Romania or Hungary," he paused and inhaled. "Still ticked off with me, Cal?

"Oh how could I be ticked off with you? I've been putting up with your idealism for nearly a century. And maybe you're right. It's no longer the dark ages. Maybe it's finally time to stop hiding in the dark."

Wilton smirked. "Thank you, *oh great and powerful master vampire.*"

"Oh just shut up, Wilton. As if seniority did get me any respect around here. The least you could do is go down to the refrigerator and get me a refill."

Wilton got up from the soft chair and took the mug off the desk, "I owe you that at least, for putting up with me. And you know what, Cal? I think Professor Garabaldi scares the hell out of his students."

"It Was Consensual"

The shipment was late. It never was before. She depended on it, for her very survival. They all did. Without it, she would surely starve; and the supply in her refrigerator was now empty. She sighed and wondered what to do.

None of her people lived close to her, so she couldn't call on them for help. She could pay someone, maybe? The nerd who worked at the all night convenience store and was always complaining that he was broke. She knew he was broke because she heard him talk about it all the time to the kid who worked the cash register, can't afford this, can't afford that, can't pay to fix the van. She looked up the number of the store and pulled her phone out of her purse and called. She thought of him first because he followed her around the store every time she was there, asking if she needed help, so it was obvious he liked her. Somehow the kid figured out her name. Must've memorized it from her credit card. Each time she came in to buy panty hose he yelled *hi Daphne* from the stock room, as if they were old friends. And he knew what she was and didn't seem to be afraid. She could afford to pay him and would offer up to five hundred cash for such easy work. That's what she planned on telling him. "No, it won't hurt too much. I'll be careful with you. You just might feel a little faint after but you'll be fine and I won't take too much"

"Hello? Is Jason there?"

"Huh? No, lady. He don't work tonight. Who's this?"

139

"Thanks. Never mind." She hung up. "Damn it." It was a dumb idea, anyway.

What was she going to do? She was beginning to feel hunger. Soon, it would become painful inside. Then she would grow weak.

It was the year 2053. The world had finally discovered them, even though they had remained well hidden for centuries. Vampires were the only ones able to survive the plagues and germ warfare unleashed upon society by extremists. They allowed their immune systems to be researched, and thus prevented the complete annihilation of humanity. All they wanted in return was to be allowed to exist in peace, no more persecution. Many people were grateful. Many were still fearful.

And some hated them with irrational rage.

She checked her e-mail for any information on where her delivery was. Half of the trucks were destroyed. Blown to bits. "What?" Humanity First claimed responsibility. There was a bomb in the parking lot where the delivery trucks were kept. It was an odd name for such a group since science had recently labeled their kind as a more highly evolved race of humanity, and the research had saved humanity from extinction. But not all people were logical. If the shipments did not arrive on time, it would cause the hunger and desperation that everyone feared in them. "How could they be so damn stupid?" And what the hell did these idiots have against shipping cattle blood across country in refrigerated trucks to people who paid for it?

She turned on the TV. It was on the news right now, what had happened earlier in the day. The leader of Humanity First was shouting to a rapt audience of his followers. "Now their evil hunger will be unleashed upon society and everyone will see the monsters they really are!" Just terrific, she thought. If anything does happen it would be the fault of those fanatics to begin with.

She turned it off and gazed out the window. The sun was slowly dimming in the sky. She would call in absent from work. She didn't feel in any shape to deal with anything tonight; she was growing weak and irritable. And soon she could become seriously dehydrated.

She decided to just walk the streets for fresh air. It might make her feel better. Maybe the delivery would come, somehow, and arrive when she got back. Or maybe not. Maybe she would collapse in the streets and be found close to starvation before dawn.

She wandered around the dark streets hoping to take her mind off her problems, but the hunger was all she could think about. She continued on.

And then she saw him. Tommy Lassiter, also known as the "neighborhood pervert." Every neighborhood had one nowadays. Creep, she thought. The guy kept getting arrested and they kept having to let him go because victims would never testify. He would say terrible things about them in court and destroy them. Decades ago, she remembered, DNA and an accusation were enough to put someone away. But after the wars, resources were so scarce, and the prisons were so full, laws changed to make justice convenient and unclog the system.

This piece of trash had been in the local papers more times than she could count. One of the many people captured and released because there was no more room to house criminals anymore, and no funds to build new facilities. On television mothers raved in front of cameras about what he had done to their children. "But it was consensual," he would always say. "Hey, like, kids are pretty grown up these days, know what I mean?" And he would go on like that, every time he was caught, and that's how he got away. It was his main defense, and remarkably, it worked. So far. People now told their kids to avoid this filth. And cops were just waiting for someone to be brave enough to do something and finally put an end to it all, but it had not happened yet.

And what was this paragon of virtue doing now? She watched. "Shit," she hissed. He was following a little kid. And what the hell was a kid doing out on his own this late? The creep was following the little boy down an alleyway. Then the kid saw him, too. And tried to run. But he was trapped. She knew this alley ended with a brick wall. She followed them, not sure what to do next.

And there he was, taking a knife out of his belt. The kid was up against the wall. "Hey, kid. I ain't gonna hurt yah. Just do what I say, and I ain't gonna hurt yah."

"Leave me alone! I'll tell!"

"You'll tell? Nobody tells! I'll tell what you did. You know what I'm gonna say? You liked it. And what are your little school friends gonna think about yah then? *Hey, what the—?"*

She leapt from behind. He was bigger than her, but she was strong, like all her kind. She was on his back, one hand of his muscular shoulder, the other in his greasy hair pulling his head back. She bit down hard. He screamed loud in her ear. But she ignored it, and drank, filling herself. She then realized he tasted horrible, as if

142

he lived off junk food and pot. But he was all that was available right now. His knees began to shake, and he sank to the ground. She held on while he went down to the pavement. He was paralyzed with shock and terror, unable to respond. All he could do was whimper. She drank until satisfied.

He collapsed, and she let go. He fell bleeding to the pavement.

She wiped her mouth, "You okay, kid?" She now remembered the boy, worried that he must be even more terrified than before.

"Hey, lady! You just saved me from that creep!"

"Well, so I did." She heard the molester moan. He was alive, but might need a transfusion. She looked at him, "If you ever, ever, say to anyone that this experience was anything but totally consensual, I will go on TV and tell the entire world how bad you wanted it. I know there are a lot of people out there with a vampire fetish. A lot! Especially these days. You followed me, and begged me for it, didn't you? And you loved it. You moaned like a male whore, which is what you are!"

The pervert looked up at her weakly and mumbled, "I really did like it."

"What?"

"Can we maybe do that again some time? Only next time with you in a French maid outfit?"

"Pig!" She kicked him where it would hurt the most. He wretched and vomited on the pavement, covering himself with filth.

She saw the boy cowering against the wall. "Are you, like real? I saw people like you on TV, but I wasn't sure if it was like a movie?"

143

"I'm real. Don't worry. I won't hurt you. Why aren't you at home with your parents?"

"They're just fightin' again. They drink, and then they start yellin' and stuff. I don't like it, so I go out and play. They don't got no food in the house, so I was gonna buy some candy. I got some change in my pockets."

"Hey, you know what? I don't have any food at home either. I bet the convenience store sells sandwiches. Come on, I'll buy you something."

"Okay!"

He took her hand, and she led him safely away into the night.

Moonlight Encounter

There weren't many of her kind left in the world. Many had been killed throughout the centuries, slaughtered in their daylight sleep by the ignorant. Butchered for what they were rather than what they did.

She sighed and looked up at the half moon. She was all alone in a castle surrounded now by wild forests, her people mostly vanished. Occasionally she met others of her kind as they traveled through the land. They would stay with her, share her hospitality, and then continue on. Sometimes they would ask her to come away with them. But no, she would say, this was her home.

She was a princess of her kind, yet outcast from the rest of humanity. Only living at night, she hunted through the forests and darkened fields. She hunted for blood.

On some nights she would see the shepherds watching over their flocks, guarding against wolves. Most were afraid of her. Sad mindless fools, she thought. She shot deer with her bow, sometimes a wild boar, or found a stray goat, the way most of her kind did. Then she would drain her quarry as it fell down dying. Or sometimes if a bandit attempted to take advantage of a lone woman wandering through the night.

She was well fed. The peasants need not worry.

She looked up at the night sky. Once her people were nearly as numerous as the stars, her father had told her. Now they were few.

She wondered if anyone would ever love her.

He gazed up at the stars and let out a sigh. His family had arranged a marriage. It was time, he was told. He had never seen the girl, but he was told that she "was from a good family," and that she was obedient. That was all. And that she could cook, and sew. She was strong and would bear many children. He did not want this, for his broken heart longed for another.

And he saw her many times, roaming the forests, this nocturnal huntress. He watched her from a far distance in the bright moonlight. He was used to finding his way in the darkness because of his many years staying awake with the flocks. By dawn he would sometimes watch her wander back to the ancient castle.

He wondered about her.

One day he went alone, not telling anyone, to see where she went to her rest. No one else had ever dared to go there, even in the light of day. He went, surprised to find an entry. No one from the village below the hills had come to this place for almost a century, and so perhaps she feared no one?

He went through and touched nothing, for he was no thief. He was only one lost man looking to find his way. There were worn but fine furnishings, tapestries, the pelts of many wild beasts, swords mounted on the grey stone walls.

And then he found her. She was beautiful. Pale and beautiful, dark blonde hair flowing over satin pillows, with lips ruby from the night before. His heart hurt with love for her, for he knew she was no demon of the night. Deep in his soul, he knew he could love her. If she would let him.

He left, but told no one.

He continued to watch her from a distance, and sometimes she would look back at him in the moonlight. She was aware of him now, yet she did nothing. She did not attack, rip out his throat, as the superstitious people said she would. She allowed him to watch her stalk her prey, from a distance, of course. This went on for some time. Often he almost got close to her, and could see her eyes flash in the moonlight. She walked through the fields on the way back to her home. Never speaking, he entertained the fantastic thought that she could one day care for him. But no. He was only a peasant.

He had been taught to read by the monks who had a monastery in the hills above the village. They educated him in payment for work done in their fields. His father and older brothers told him he was foolish, that he should have taken the money that was offered instead. But when he took his sheep to market he would spend a few coins on a book or two before he left town to return to his small farm. His family felt this useless habit of books was a waste of both pennies and time. Still, he read of legends from faraway lands, poetry, tales of gods and warriors long forgotten, even the writings of great philosophers. He read by the light of the fire on nights that he did not see his dark princess so he would not be totally alone.

He was the only one in the village who could read.

The moon was full that night. It was the night before his bride was to be brought to his village to be prepared for marriage. Then his fate would be sealed. He would marry and he would continue to tend his sheep, and his wife would obediently cook, clean, and sew. She would obediently lie under him and bear his children. Then after many years of hard work his life would come to an end. He was to be quickly married, yet remain alone in the world.

Sadly, he looked around the meadow to see if the vampiress was anywhere nearby. There she was, sitting on a large rock where the meadow met the forest, watching him. Perhaps she was curious about him also?

He had to act now, for tomorrow would be too late. Forgive me, his whispered.

She saw the young man slowly approach. Finally, she thought, after so many nights, he is to come. And what did he want? She wondered. Now she would find out. But it couldn't be that, could it?

He came closer to her. She sat on the rock that had in ancient times been part of a stone barrier at the edge of the forest and watched him. He came to her looking fearful but hopeful. Then before her, he knelt and took her hand, and kissed it. He reached up to open the top of his shirt and silently she bent to his throat. He trembled as she bit down, and he let out a soft cry. He put his arms around her as she quietly drank. Together they felt each other's warmth on a cold dark night. They fell down into the tall cool grass and held each other. She drank little yet her love consumed him. For a moment in time it seemed the movement of the earth and stars ceased, and nothing existed but their embrace.

As he grew weaker she released him and sat up, "I did not know any mortal man would ever come to me like you did. Why?"

He reach up to touch her dark golden hair. "I don't know why. I only know you've taken my heart."

She bent to kiss him. He tasted his own blood on her lips. "You've taken mine as well, yet I do not even know your name."

"Owen."

"Alessandra."

They rested on the grass and gazed at the starlit sky above. Slowly he began to talk about himself and confessed his love of books and poetry. He told of his family, and how they did not understand him. Then he sadly told her of tomorrow. "They will bring her before me, and I must accept her. Then the marriage will be set for before the harvest. I do not know this woman, but it is our way." He had read tales of foreign lands where marriage was for love, but that was not in the life of his small village.

"When next the moon is this bright, you will gain your strength back. Come to the castle, and there you will find many fine old books."

The sun was coming into the sky. She left.

He came then into the castle and found it warmly lit with the glow of the large fire in the hearth. She had prepared venison for him. He ate and she talked of her people long ago, and how many of her family were killed off during the day while they slept. It made him sad to hear it.

"And so what of your family?" she asked.

"They are furious that I did not give my answer. I told them I wanted to marry for love. My father blasted me, saying that too many useless books have put ideas into my head, and that I was acting above myself, and that I had better decide to marry her and be quick about it, for he was promised two pigs and a cow by her father, and so on."

She laughed and took his hand, "Come then, read to me from some useless book. For I have many." She told him to pick one from the shelf, and he sat there by the fire and read tales of knights and heroes and ancient lands. She reclined on the bearskin rug in front of the hearth, closed her eyes and listened as he read on.

She interrupted his story, "And so did the hero marry the princess?"

"I don't know. I haven't come to the end of it."

"Do you think he would?" she asked.

"Of course he would. For he loves her, with all his heart, and would surely die without her. Do you think she would have him?"

"I think she would," she pulled him close. He dropped the book; it landed on the fur rug. "Do they know about us?"

"I really don't care." He untied the top of his linen shirt. "Take your pleasure from me, Princess."

She bit into him; he moaned softly and shivered. He held onto her to steady himself, and he stroked her long golden hair as she drank. He soon collapsed from ecstasy and she let him down onto the rug.

She ran a white finger across his throat, caressing his small wound.

"I wish we could be together, always and forever," he said.

"Is that what you truly want?"

"Yes," he whispered, "To be with you. Forever."

The daylight came and the young shepherd never returned. Most in the village claimed that the vampiress took him away with her into the darkness, drained his blood, and made him like herself.

Some, however, whispered that he ran away to be with a secret lover.

Dark Angel

They were almost at their destination, finally. Six year old Tracy was still asleep on the backseat of the Escalade. It had taken her all day and half the night to stop crying hysterically. But he drove on, not stopping to comfort her. He had to keep driving. He couldn't stop running. The girl was innocent. And now she was a witness.

Even if he managed to keep them both alive long enough to survive and escape, he might not have long himself, without treatment. But he couldn't think about that now. The road went on, an endless stream of darkness, and he could not get the terrible sound out of his head. The sound of the blast kept echoing in his shattered mind all the way down the road. The car bomb in the Mercedes was meant for him. But it took Laverne's life. His wife was always against him taking the job. But working for Gambini paid big. Why didn't he listen? Why didn't he stick with his dull accounting job instead of becoming a bookkeeper for the mob? And now, he just knew too much.

And he kept driving. There was no looking back. His wife was gone. He had to save himself, save their little girl. He just hoped that Valentino "The Boss" Gambini didn't know about the cabin his grandfather kept deep in the woods. They had ways of finding things out. They could search public land records. Or did he let it slip out one day about Gramp's old hunting cabin? Yeah, it's a great place to get away from it all.

There wouldn't be a hospital anywhere near where he was going, because soon he would need one. Either a hospital, or a small clinic. Hell, even a veterinarian would do. The illness was always in the back of his mind. But he couldn't worry about it. He needed to keep driving until they got away.

It was nearly dawn when he arrived. Nothing but silence surrounded the cabin, and the few remaining stars hovered above the trees. He left the few pieces of luggage he quickly packed, picked his daughter up off the backseat and carried her in, still fast asleep. The cabin had only three rooms, a bedroom, a small sitting room, and an even smaller kitchen. There was a primitive bathroom, with a shower he hoped was still working properly. Hell, all that really mattered now was that Gambini's men didn't find the place.

He gently placed the girl on the couch and stood up, and the dizziness came. It wasn't much, so he ignored it. But he knew. It was starting. He refused to think about it. Instead he would try to get some sleep.

Polycythemia vera. The name for his condition echoed in his brain as he laid his head down. Tracy didn't need to lose both of her parents right now. But what the hell was he going to do? If Gambini didn't get him, then that would. His body produced way too many red blood cells than it needed. Without treatment, it would clog the vessels, eventually give him a heart attack or stroke. Treatment was simple enough, just donate at the Red Cross every so often. But what would he do out in the middle of nowhere? Maybe if he found a knife he could treat it himself? But that would be dangerous and stupid. Just like working for Gambini was dangerous and stupid.

153

As he drifted slowly off to sleep, he realized, the symptoms were returning.

She drifted through the darkened forest simply wanting to complete her mission and return home. But her uncle Janek's words kept echoing in her mind. *Every vampire must learn to hunt. It is your destiny.* He insisted she learn to fend for herself, just like back in the old country, even in these comfortable well-fed modern times with refrigerators full of bottled animal blood. He insisted that she go out into the night, listen to the silence, perceive the whisper of distant hoof beats of a stag upon the moss covered ground, follow, stalk, kill and feed.

She'd rather be at home surfing the internet or watching cable. But she knew her uncle was right. She needed to learn to be self-sufficient, and so she continued on.

Her uncle kept one of the cabins clustered around Hidden Lake. Usually this time of year the other cabins were empty. Strangely, though, she noticed she was not alone. She could see lights on in the cabin across the water. Whoever they were, they came three nights ago. She hungered, inhaled the cool night air, and continued her hunt.

Three days and nights, he figured it was. And his head was getting fuzzy, he knew. And he started to feel tired all the time again. Why now, of all times, when he needed to be strong enough to either protect himself and his little girl, if and when they came, or at least be quick enough to escape? He had to get up, prepare food for himself and

154

Tracy, but even that was an effort. He considered finding a knife to slice his wrist, but what good would that do if he couldn't manage to stop it once it started? Gambini would have people watching all the hospitals within a five hundred mile radius, he imagined, since he was stupid enough to once tell them of his condition.

He slept uneasily. Every sound in the trees, every birdcall to him sounded like Gambini's men approaching. Soon the food he bought at a convenience store while on the run would be gone. What would he do then? Try and catch fish in the lake? Yeah, right. A city guy like him, trying to live off the land? That was a real joke. If he caught a fish he hadn't the slightest idea how to prepare it. In his exhausted state he could hear Old Gramp's voice echo through his tired head, "You're gonna grow up to be soft, boy. Your momma ought to let me take yah huntin' and fishin' one a these days."

She listened, hearing only the sound of the wind in the trees. A rustle in the bushes, maybe a rabbit? She could catch that, satisfy her hunger, be done with it, and return to her cabin, sleep the day then return to her people. Too late. It had already gone. She listened. Suddenly there was a faint wail from across the water. She turned to look towards the lake. The moon's light painted the dark water silver. Beyond there was the other cabin, the only other inhabitants of the forest besides the animals. She listened again, and heard the sound of tears, the sound of a child sobbing helplessly.

It took nearly an hour to walk the path around the lake to get to the other side and reach the other cabin. When she arrived, there was nothing but silence and darkness. A dim light glowed from a front window. Cautiously, she knocked at the door. It slowly opened. She looked down to see a little girl, her eyes red from crying.

"My Daddy's real sick. He said not to let any of the guys he works with in. But you don't look like any of them."

"What's wrong with your Daddy?"

"He's got this weird disease where he's got too much blood and he'll get a heart attack if he don't give some. The doctor said so."

"Too much?" She had heard of the condition. It had a long name she could not quite remember. Her uncle told her about it once, laughing about how convenient it would be if it were more common. "Well, are you sure that's what's wrong with him?"

"The doctor said he needs to give blood or he'll die soon, and there's no hospitals nearby. He said we have to stay here, 'cause of the bad people who killed Mommy."

This girl's story just gets sadder and sadder. She didn't even know if any of it were true. "Well, maybe I know how to help your father. Stay here." She slowly drifted into the bedroom and found him nearly unconscious, flat on his back. He looked up at her and whispered something incoherent. She slowly opened the collar of his shirt, gave his throat a gentle soft caress, and sat beside him.

Barely alert, he gazed at her with half open eyes, as though he thought she must be a dream. She smiled slightly at the thought, and bent closer. "Don't worry," she whispered, "I won't hurt you." He cried out suddenly as she bit down, piercing his flesh. She quietly drank as the blood rushed to her lips. Too weak to struggle, he made a futile attempt at pushing her off. She reached to hold down his arms, keeping him immobile, and continued to drink.

He awakened slowly in the darkness. It was one hell of a crazy dream he had. Must have been a combination of seeing his wife blown to bits, running from Gambini, and the illness. And it was all too real. In fact, he realized, his neck even hurt slightly.

Voices coming from the kitchen.

Who the hell was Tracy talking to out there? If it were one of that murdering bastard's men, he wasn't even strong enough to get up and do something about it. He listened. "Daddy said the bomb was really for him, 'cause he knew too much, and the FBI wanted to talk to him. He said we had to run. He wouldn't even let me go back to get my bear. I miss Mommy."

"I wish I could change that. But don't worry, your Daddy will be all right now. He'll be better, after getting some rest."

"Are you really for real? I seen people like you on TV."

"Of course I'm real. But vampires aren't anything like what you see on TV. Everything you see on TV is completely wrong."

Oh cripes, he thought. Either he was still dreaming, or Gambini had vampires on his payroll, which wasn't likely, since he did the payroll, and he knew all of Gambini's employees, which included everything from hit men to hookers.

"Most of us live on animal blood, but you said your father needed help, and since I was here . . ." She went on answering questions matter-of-factly, as if she were speaking to a miniature adult. He stayed quiet and got an earful, as he learned to do at his former job. The girl kept asking questions, and so he learned the dream's name was Clara and she was about fifty-five years old, although he recalled she appeared to be about nineteen. Hell, she didn't only look nineteen, she looked like Audrey Hepburn in blue jeans.

So then, he realized, he must be dreaming this whole scenario. None of it could be real, he thought. He never took the job for Gambini. He was still in his dead end job and his wife was still alive, not blown to bits, and they were still struggling to pay the damn mortgage. So he drank too much last night, and dreamed the entire last four and a half miserable years of his rotten life, starting with working for the mob, and ending with being bitten by a vampire who looked like Audrey Hepburn.

"Most of the time, Tracy, we live just like everyone else. We work, we pay bills; we do laundry. But we can't spend too much time in the sun. I sleep most of the day, but not in a coffin like you see in movies. I wake up at dusk and get blood out of my refrigerator." Tracy went on excitedly asking all sorts of questions, with the same curiosity and lack of fear she would show when asking a neighbor boy about his new puppy. Clara wasn't repelled by any religious items either, and neither were any of her fellow vampires; that was all made up too. And they didn't live forever, only "three hundred years, maybe a little more," because, she said, they aged very slowly. And no, Daddy won't become a vampire just because she bit him. "But he really ought to take better care of his condition so he doesn't need a vampire to come every time he gets sick like that. You know, we're busy too, and we can't all be making house calls—"

"But it would be cool if he would be a vampire, because then he could just fly away from the bad men!"

"That doesn't happen in real life either, Tracy."

It was late morning when he woke up. He tried to move but felt stiff. And his neck still hurt, slightly. It was one hell of a realistic dream. Too bad his real life was becoming a nightmare. He struggled up out of bed, still wearing the clothes he wore the night before, and shuffled out to the small kitchen.

"Look, Daddy, look!"

"What is it, Tracy?"

"She brought food!"

"What?" He saw bags of groceries on the countertop.

"I told her everything that you like and then she went out to get it, 'cause you made us leave so fast we didn't take anything."

There was a box of Tracy's favorite sugar coated cereal, and box of the small chocolate donuts she always begged for, frozen waffles, Tracy's favorite cookies, and a big bag of marshmallows. "What? Where did all this stuff come from?"

"Clara brought it last night while you were getting better." She looked up at him and smiled brightly. "I told her all the stuff you like to eat, Daddy!"

"No. This is stuff you like to eat, honey. Look, now someone knows we're here," and it dawned on him that maybe he wasn't dreaming. His life was steadily getting worse. His wife was blown to bits by the mafia, he was on the run from the mob, and he was bitten by a vampire who returned with bags full of junk food, but no beer.

"Where is Clara right now, honey?"

"She's asleep Daddy, 'cause it's daytime."

His mind spun around with the concept. Was last night real? Or not? Did vampires exist? Impossible. But then again, some people didn't believe the mafia existed either. Then he noticed the stuffed toy kitten on the countertop behind the grocery bags. It was new, and still had tags on it. "Where did that come from, Tracy?"

"Clara brought that too," she said. "Because you made me leave without my bear. Can she come back and visit us, Daddy? I like her."

"Tracy. *She's a—*" he almost couldn't say it. She's a vampire. But then he told himself it wasn't real, couldn't be real. That would be ridiculous. It must have been some girl staying at a cabin nearby, and she heard the little girl crying while he was too sick to comfort his own little girl. He heard her come in, he heard her talking to Tracy, and then he must have passed out and dreamed the rest. "Sure honey. She can come visit." After all, the mafia had just butchered his wife while trying to finish him off. And they wouldn't give up until they succeeded. He had more important things to worry about than whether or not vampires were real. "Honey, next time a strange lady comes to visit in the middle of the night, tell her to bring a six pack, okay?"

For the rest of the afternoon he ate peanut butter sandwiches because peanut butter was one of the items that Tracy suggested to Clara, and watched the small television that sat on the countertop in the kitchenette, watching various nonsense until late in the day, wondering what to do next. He had no time to mourn for Laverne. He would wait until they were finally free from Gambini. Eventually, he knew, they would catch up to him. He needed to decide where they would go next. They couldn't stay at the cabin forever.

He also wondered about Clara. Who was she? *What was she?* Did she work for Gambini? Probably not, or else he'd already be dead, like Laverne.

A tear drifted slowly down his cheek. Quickly he wiped it away. He needed to be strong for Tracy. If Gambini's men came for them, they would need to make a run for it. Again. He would need to grab Tracy and start running again. Maybe they'd both be running for the rest of their lives. He imagined the future, him getting old and Tracy a young woman, still drifting from place to place, living on the road, doing odd jobs until finally Gambini caught up with them. Then it dawned on him. Where the hell was Tracy?

"Tracy?" No answer. Oh God. *Where the hell was Tracy?*

Night was finally beginning to arrive. The skies were growing dark, and the air was growing cool. The night birds began their song while the wind whispered through the trees. Slowly and softly she stirred awake.

It was dusk. She inhaled quietly, realizing that it would soon be time to return home to her people, her mission complete. *I did what you said, Uncle.*

She had finally gotten around to using the crossbow he handed to her after his long talk on their great ancient hunting traditions and his lecture on her need for

161

survival skills, shot an arrow into a rabbit, and drank blood from its dying body. And she felt grief ever since. She would get over it, of course. She was glad she didn't destroy a majestic stag or some other creature that she felt was just too beautiful.

She had lived on the blood of domestic cattle raised for that purpose, kept on farms owned by her people, they were drained of only a little at a time and never slaughtered. She never saw the farms, of course. She only saw the interior of her refrigerator. And then there was the occasional "volunteer" – those who were fascinated by vampires and who sought them out. As long as things were kept secretive and discreet, it was allowed.

She rose to get ready to leave. She would shower, dress, and gather her things to bring out to her car. Filled with both the blood of the rabbit and the man whose life she most likely saved and who was now probably ungrateful for being bitten and thinking that he had been savaged by some fabled monster, she knew she wouldn't need much for the long road home. There was a tapping sound at her door, "What?" She opened it quickly. *"Tracy?"*

"Last night you said you were at a cabin across the lake. It took a real long time to get to here. I walked the whole way round the lake. I knew this one was yours, 'cause there was a car here but it was quiet like you were sleeping. So I waited."

"Tracy? What are you doing here? Your father will be worried about you!"

"I know. I was hoping you could come stay with us. He'll get sick again. He always does, and there's no hospitals out in the woods."

She took the little girl's hand and pulled her inside and closed the door, "Now Tracy, look, first, I have to go home soon, and second, most people really don't like people like me hanging around."

"Why not?" she whined.

"Well, most people don't like vampires. That's why."

"How come?"

"Because of all the bad things you see on TV. Now look, I'm bringing you right back to your father."

"And then can you stay with us?"

"No, Tracy. I'm sorry. He won't want me to stay. I told you that."

She held the little girl's hand as she led her through the forest toward the other side of the lake. Clara needed only the light of the moon and stars to guide her. Down the path that led around the lake, the little girl continued to pester her with questions and she patiently answered them, "No. I really can't communicate telepathically with wolves. That's just on TV," she sighed. "Children are filled with all sorts of questions. I suppose you want to know why the sky is blue."

"No. Who cares about that?"

"Well, in case you were about to ask, I don't know why. And I don't care either. I just want to bring you home to your father." And so they walked on, working their way around the starlit lake until they got closer to the cabin where Tracy's father was hiding.

Tracy kept on talking, on and on about how her mother was blown to bits, and Dad won't say anything, but he thinks the bomb was really meant for him, and these people called FBI wanted to find him. "What's FBI mean?"

"Tracy, shhh!" She put her hand over the little girl's mouth and whispered, "There's a car coming down the road toward the cabin."

The road was far off, and though Tracy knew the road came up to the cabin, she could not see it in the dark.

"I hear it. There is a car, coming up the road, without its lights on."

"Why would they have the lights off?" she pulled Clara's hand away.

"So no one can see them coming, that's why! Stay here, Tracy."

It was dark, and she was missing. He had searched the cabin, under the beds, in the closets; and she was nowhere. He was going out to find her. He grabbed his leather jacket and flung the door open.

And there right in front of him was Joey Barbarino, one of Gambini's men.

"Did yah miss us?" Joey smiled. "You didn't come to work so the boss was all worried about yah! He thought yah might a got sick with that weird illness!"

"Hey, now listen, Joey."

But Joey didn't have a chance to reach for his gun. Instead he was pulled down from behind. The motion was too swift and silent for him to see. *"What the—?"* Next he saw Joey was on the ground with Clara's fangs in his throat. Joey put up a good struggle, but eventually sank into unconsciousness.

"Oh Christ!"

She turned to him, and in the semi-darkness he saw blood dripping from her lips, "Well, what did you want me to do? Let him shoot you?"

"Daddy! Daddy!" The little girl came bounding happily out of the forest.

"Tracy!" He ran and picked her up.

"Clara saved your Daddy! Can she stay with us? Please? Can she?"

Clara's apartment was small but comfortable. There were no cobwebs, no caskets, no bats, no capes in the closets—he had already checked while she was out. The only thing that showed any difference was what was in the refrigerator.

"These documents are the closest to the real thing as anyone can get," she said. "Uncle Janek has some very creative people. When you don't age, or if you're discovered, you sometimes just need to reinvent yourself, disappear, start over, or become someone else," she paused, "You know, we don't often do this, for . . . for others."

"Yeah. I figured." He looked at the new driver's license, passport, and social security card: Nathaniel S. Henderson. That was who he was now. He was still an accountant, there was even a college degree from a school he had never heard of, but he was certain no one would bother to check references. They almost never did. "Clara. I just don't know how to thank you, and your Uncle Janek, for helping us like this."

"Of course, you can thank us by keeping quiet about us. Remember, like you, we are forever being hunted."

But Joey knew. She had left him alive, to stumble around the dark forest when he finally got his strength back. Gambini would take care of him, though. The boss didn't like mistakes. He got his jacket and headed out the door pulling Tracy along by the hand. They were on their way to as far as they could get from Gambini. He had enough cash with him to find a place to stay, and start over.

Tracy broke away and ran to wrap her arms around Clara, "I'll miss you, Clara."

Clara stroked her straw colored hair, "Go on now, and be safe."

"Will we ever see you ever again?"

"Well," she sighed, "I really don't believe that Uncle Janek would want two people out there in the world who knew about us, without having someone check up on you, once in a while." Then she smiled mysteriously and looked at Nathaniel. "And of course, you will need someone to look after your health. Won't you?"

My Cousin from New Jersey

L ike, you guys gonna shoot me? 'Cause if you are, it's still not gonna change nothin'. It won't, okay? And I said I won't tell the damn tabloids, it's too embarrassing. It really is. Why do you need a tape recorder, anyway? I told this crap five hundred times to you people! Why don't you just leave me alone, let me go home to clean up my place and feed my poor dog? I told you. I told you! I don't know where it is! All right, fine, here it is. One more time.

Yeah. Okay, like I said, it was the night that the stupid TV reported that something, a glowing object, crashed. And, yeah, like I said, it shook the floor when it hit. Yeah. So what? So? I told you guys. Yeah, I saw it come down. Then the TV interrupts the Star Trek rerun to say that it's only a meteorite or some stupid thing. I was mad, 'cause I wait all day for that show to come on. How come you military people had to make them interrupt my show? I was real pissed off. I work all day, I wanna come home and space out in front of my show. Okay, okay. Take it easy. Hey don't point that thing at me.

So at one in the morning, the dog was barking, real loud. I was pissed off 'cause I had to get up and go to my so-called job and the old lady I rent the lousy four rooms from hates the noise. So like I said, I went out and the garage door was open when I got out and the dog was freaking out and all hysterical, barking into the garage. The lights were on in there, which was weird, because I know I shut them off.

Anyway, there he was, the poor little guy was hiding under my '69 Chevelle. Hey, that's a good car. I'm real mad that you put a bullet hole in it. I guess you guys won't pay to fix it, will yah? Yup. I figured as much. So much for where my taxes go. Anyway, the poor thing was under the engine. Yeah, at first I was scared because his eyes were glowing in the dark under there and stuff, but he looked scared, so I felt bad. So I coaxed the little guy out. His silver space suit was all torn up, too. He looked all roughed up. He just crawled out and leaned against the wall. Shaking too.

So I went in the house and brought a blanket. I didn't want him in, 'cause before I got to know him better I thought he was kinda spooky, yah know?

Anyhow, the next morning—and I did not sleep at all—no! Anyway, around dawn I started to feel bad again about this. Like, I figured, he's in a strange place and he's probably hurt and all that. So it was just barely dawn, with gray light just coming up into the dark sky. I got up and looked out the window and looked down into the valley. I could still see the smoke from the crash and see flashing lights and hear the sirens. Down on the highway below the jeeps and trucks were still coming and going like crazy. Then I felt scared again, but not of what was in the garage.

He was still there, sitting in the corner with the blanket wrapped around him, staring down at the cement floor looking miserable. So I asked him if he wanted to come in. What else was I gonna do? He looked up at me, no expression at all on his little gray face; slowly he got up, and followed me in.

He really freaked out the dog at first, but the mutt calmed down after a while. I had to go to work too, to my so called job. So I told him I was going to work, I didn't know if he would understand what work was, or even if he was able to understand anything I said. But what the hell, I left him in the house with the dog. Just to relieve my own tension I figured I would try and say something cute so I said there's beer and stuff in the fridge. I tried to laugh. I couldn't. He just stood there gazing at me with those dark red glowing eyes of his. I got real scared when he looked at me like that. Then I left.

When I got home, oh hell. What a bad trip. I never saw anybody get Americanized so fast. The TV was on. Like, the first thing he discovered about Earth must have been the TV control. Quite a big discovery too! And when I came in, there he was, sitting on the couch, surrounded by empty cans. There was an empty corn chip bag on the floor, and he had a big bowl of pretzels on the couch next to him. He turned to look at me, and smiled happily, and said, "Honey! I'm home!"

"W-hat?" I said. "What did you say?"

He smiled again, with his dark almond shaped eyes shining in the glow of the television, "Nine out of ten doctors and their lawyers recommend Luxe Fabric Softener!"

So then I began to really worry. Like, either the poor little guy was seriously injured in the crash. Or he watched too much useless crap on TV. But it didn't matter. 'Cause then I tried to ignore him while I checked the phone messages, and, oh my God, they were all confirming about the party that I had forgotten with all the excitement. Now I started thinking fast. How was I gonna hide him now? I was gonna have like twenty people coming over Saturday night. Hopefully they would be all too drunk to notice. Then the last message came on. It was cousin Myron from New Jersey. He couldn't make it. He had been arrested again. Shit. He'll never learn. I told him to quit selling to undercover cops, but he don't listen. None of my friends had ever met Myron, but they all knew about him because I talked about him a lot. They just knew that he was pale and little, weird, and kinda spaced out. It was too bad he couldn't make it to the party, I hadn't seen him in years. Ordinarily I'd be totally upset about that, but mainly I was just worried about that one thing. I couldn't get it out of my head: How was I going to hide a space alien with the damned FBI and the CIA and the IRS outside and twenty stoned idiots inside? It was gonna be a rough weekend.

"Don't worry! It will be okay! We're here for you! Just tell our audience how long you have been a transvestite child-molesting alcoholic lesbian pimp weighing three hundred and ninety nine pounds and who claims to have been abducted by O.J. Simpson, and could it all be just due to low self-esteem?"

I wanted to scream. I really, really did. But I had to keep it all together. "Okay," I said, "Look, you gotta help me here." And then I started to think of a real crazy plan.

So we went to the supermarket. Yeah. That's right. We went to the supermarket. We went first to a thrift shop to get him some street clothes. He looked like everybody else then, I suppose. Hat on the wrong way, baggy jeans with lotsa holes in them, an ugly sweat shirt ten sizes too big, and one of those choke chain dog collars. Yeah. That's right. The kids in the neighborhood wear them.

Think it's real cool. So then we went to the supermarket. He picked up a lot of the kinda stuff he cleaned me out of already. Chips, nachos, pretzels, cheeze dings and stuff like that, the nutritious stuff, you know. He reminded me to get the beer. It was good he did, because he had cleaned out all that too.

So we get home and what does he do? He drops on the couch again and grabs the TV control again. Yeah. So after I put stuff away I figured I had no choice. After all, he was an advanced being. I got a bowl of cheese dings and a six pack and sat myself down. The Jessie Jones Show was good that day, I remember.

Then at seven they all came. It was an invasion. Like, twice the number of people I expected came. Myron, that's what his name would be now, he loved it. He loved all the people, no kidding. People were all captivated by his outgoing personality and lighthearted smile. Everyone would go introduce themselves, start up conversations. And he was great at conversation now that he knew a lot about our culture.

"Hey man, we heard a lot about you! What's been happening to you these days?" So he goes, "I've fallen and I can't get up!"

"Hey, Myron, yo dude! How yah been?"

He smiles and he says, "Dy-No-Mite!"

"So, it's Myron, huh? Is it true about the drug bust last week?"

"What you talkin 'bout, Willis?"

Then this spaced out broad who walked in with some of the guys I knew who told me her name was Robin, she came on to him. "Hey. I been with a lotta guys in every way possible. But somehow you just seem, like, different.

171

Wanna go someplace together after this dull party?" He didn't quite grasp the concept, though, "Quick Robin! To the Bat Cave!"

He loved the music too. They all brought their collection of Metalhead CD's; someone brought a strobe light. He had been watching MTV so he knew how to dance real well. It was a cool party scene. I was just happy to see the little guy have a good time so many light years away from his real home. Someone brought the weed out so he learned all about that too. Made him real happy. In the darkness I saw his eyes glow from red to purple; when he finally started smoking he began to levitate up several inches, maybe almost a foot, up off the couch he was on.

Somehow, I wasn't surprised by all that. But the funny thing about it was, even though his eyes glowed in the dark and he was floating in the air and mumbling in some strange alien foreign language, none of the other people seemed to notice it much. To them, maybe it seemed just normal.

Then I heard this big roaring noise overhead. I was the only one sober so no one else noticed, except maybe Myron. I figured it was a military helicopter. I could tell he was getting upset when he started acting hysterical. He pointed up at the ceiling and yelled, "The plane! The plane!"

But everyone kept on dancing.

Then these guys in fatigues and carrying machine guns busted down my door. The guys all just figured it was cops and they ran to the john to flush their stuff. Then in comes these serious people in dark suits, "We have had reports of an alien at this location," one of them said in this dull, real dead monotone that I figured was typical of most government officials.

The people did not comprehend so they began to protest: "Hey man, like, we're all American citizens!" And, "Yeah, like, I got a green card!"

The government agents kept looking around the room but everyone looked the same, including Myron. Really. He looked and acted just like everyone else in those thrift shop rags and untied sneakers and dog collar I got for him. I saw him in among the crowd, trying real hard to blend in, act casual. He was talking again with the chick who wanted to do him earlier, "If you've been hurt or injured in an accident or on the job, you deserve to get what's coming to you!"

They searched the place with the armed men watching us to make sure nobody moved. They searched the john but only found the drugs people didn't flush quick enough. They searched my closet but only found more clothes from more thrift stores. And my old guitar. And a bunch of empty beer cans. They searched my bedroom but only found my dog and my collection of comic books and the pile of clothes and stuff that's always on the floor anyway. They searched the laundry room but I don't do no laundry so they didn't find anything in there. They searched the kitchen but only found the last bag of corn chips and a single can of beer. They got mad and demanded to know where the alien was!

I could tell Myron was scared. Real scared. Like, he was over in the dark corner, clutching the TV control, clicking at the men in suits, trying to make them all disappear. He couldn't figure out why the channel wouldn't change like it always had for him before, ever since he crash landed.

Then one of the gun totting jerks notices and screams out like a maniac, "Watch out! It's got a weapon!" And the idiots rush in with guns firing, it was a war zone, everybody hits the deck, I went down to the floor, then I was sorry I hadn't vacuumed the purple shag carpet for like, I dunno, ten years.

After the noise quieted down, I looked up. There he was, fallen, lifeless on the floor in the corner of the room. Robin was crying, then I noticed that I was crying too. I couldn't stand it. I really couldn't. My head just went down into the stinky old rug and I cried uncontrollably. It really hurt. It really got me. One minute he was having a real good time, and then. Then he was dead.

And then you guys drag me and all my friends in here, put a bullet hole in my Chevy, lock up my dog in the bathroom just 'cause he's barkin'. Didn't you guys do enough by killing my little friend? Huh? You have to make us all damn miserable too?

And to finish it all, you dissect him. And then you go telling me there is nothing, nothing, nothing in his skull but this strange-weird-gray-jello-sticky-liquid-oatmeal-crap? You keep on asking me were the hell his brain is? 'Cause you wanna study it? Well, I do not know! Okay? I don't! I told you everything. That's how it all happened! Really! He landed on earth, he got relaxed, he watched TV, sat on the couch, drank some beer, ate some corn chips and pretzels, patted the dog, watched more TV, drank some more beer, saw a talk show then watched MTV, had fun at the party, drank some more beer, danced with all the chicks, smoked a little weed.

And that's all that happened! We do not know what happened to Myron's brain. We really do not.

Are you gonna let me go now?

Warning Signs

"**K**ill. Kill. Kill." He drove down the street, passively chanting in his usual dull lifeless and robotic monotone, "Kill. Kill. Kill."

"Like, what is wrong with you that you talk that way?" I finally asked.

"Nothing. I'm just a normal guy. I'm a man. I need to kill. Men need to kill," he quietly explained. And he continued on, chanting the word "kill" while driving. There was no emotion in his voice, nor was he driving recklessly. He simply repeated the word "kill" over and over again, like his own personal prayer to his inner darkness.

I was nineteen and not very worldly, but I knew something must be wrong, although I did not know what. He wanted me to marry him. He kept asking me to—no, *he kept ordering me*—to marry him. He would not accept no for an answer and there was no discussion. He had my future planned for me, without my input or consent.

I would quit college, and quit my job. I would never work again, he told me. I was to stay home, and "just be a wife." We would move to Alabama, and live in a trailer, and he would hunt, to "live off the land." Sometimes the plan was different. We would move to New Hampshire and have a farm, with cows. Whenever he talked of the imaginary farm that he would have in the future, he emphasized that there would be "cows." And he wanted us to have twins, "twin little girls," he would say, with an odd look on his face.

He suddenly stopped chanting "kill" and started it up again, about how we were going to be married soon, and all about his plans.

"I think I really should finish college first, okay?" I would say that, figuring that in the time it took to finish college, he'd get bored with me and get interested in something, or someone, else.

"No wife a mine gonna go to no college. You're gonna do what you're told, and marry me."

"Yah know, if you keep talking to me that way, I might leave you. I don't like the way you talk to me all the time."

He pulled up into my driveway, "You can't leave me. You need me. You can't live five minutes without me. You'll just come crawling back."

"Need you for what? My life was fine before I met you, and it will be fine after you're gone." I was getting mad, like I always did. Looking back, I wonder if he liked getting me mad? I got out, slammed the door. "I'm going to go to college, and do something with my life, and you're not gonna stop me."

"I told you not to slam the door on my truck!" He suddenly exploded. It was one of the few times he raised his voice. It surprised me. He finally got upset. Over his cheap old truck.

"Yeah. Okay. Bye."

I never had any intention of marrying him. It was all his idea. The entire relationship, I began to see, was all in his head. He was in a hurry to marry, start a family, and in the process, stop the course of my life, or at least take control of it. He was determined to bend me to his will, change my personality, to transform me into his fantasy of what I should be. He sometimes called me "Mommy" instead of by my name. And sometimes, he just called me "dumb female."

I didn't know what drove him. I didn't know that much about him, other than that he was adopted and that he was in the Army. He loved the Army. And he loved guns.

I knew it would never work out. We always ended up disagreeing. He had very out of date beliefs, such as that women should not go to college, or drive cars, or have careers. Career women, he said, just used their bodies to get ahead, because women have no other ability. Most unusual, he wanted to go to war, "to kill," he said. "I hope we have a war, so I can kill. I want to kill." He promised me that if he killed the enemy, "I'll bring back his boots for you."

I was only nineteen, but I knew something just wasn't right with him. I had no idea why he was in such a hurry to get married. He wanted to get married "now," he would often say.

He never talked much when he wasn't talking about "killing" or "war," but in conversation he frequently repeated in his usual dull monotone that he "loved" me. There was never any emotion in these words, and his face would be dead and cold and expressionless as he said them. Anything else he would say to me or about me would involve criticism, about my clothes, my hair, my jewelry, my friends, my favorite music, my reading "stupid books," or about "girls going to college."

At one point he began introducing me to his friends as "the girl he was going to marry." I would whisper, *"I never said I would marry you."*

"You will," he said coldly, "Don't worry. *You will.*"

178

After that day, after slamming shut the door of his truck, I decided to give up on him. He would never change. And neither would I. I could never become what he wanted me to be. I needed to do something with my life, and make my own decisions.

He kept calling. I refused to answer the phone. Friends criticized brutally, he was "such a great guy," they said. I was stupid, they said, to leave him like that. They were never alone with him, like I was. They didn't know what he was about, really. They saw the flowers and gifts he gave me, but they never heard the frequent criticism that eventually evolved into death threats. They never heard him say, "I have a gun, and I know how to use it." He never caused me any harm, for which I am lucky. In fact, he never put a hand on me.

His words were terrifying enough.

Decades passed by. I got my associate degree, then went nights and got my Bachelor of Science degree. The war against terror began, and he probably got his wish, to go to war, so he could kill. More time went by and I had a career change after being downsized, so I got a third college degree. I have a career. I've traveled to the Rocky Mountains, to Europe and North Africa. I control my own money, and basically live life the way I choose to. People say they feel sorry for me, and what a terrible pity that I've never married.

If they only knew, I'm lucky to just be alive, to have escaped without having my mind broken and my soul devoured.

I think of him from time to time and wonder about him, and wonder if he had some sort of undiagnosed mental illness, or some sort of autism. His family did not seem well educated, so perhaps, I wondered, he was never encouraged to seek any help? That maybe his adoptive parents would just ignore his behavior, thinking his backwardness was somehow normal?

Or perhaps those were just his attitudes? But out of date attitudes do not explain the cold dead sound of the monotone of his voice, the dull look in his ice-cold eyes, his endless fascination with killing and death and war.

I heard he got married, and worry that he might be abusive to his wife and family. But I will never know the answers. Somehow, I really just don't want to know.

I don't think about the past that much, but every once in a while I realize there are many others who went in the opposite direction, and didn't listen to the voice inside, the voice that says, *Get out before it's too late.*

And sometimes I wonder what my life would be like if I did quit college and do what I was told, get married, stay home, and just be a wife?

I meet a friend for coffee. She is going through a vicious divorce. Her eyes are moist and red, her face is pale, and she has lost weight. Her hands shake as she talks. I take out my mirror and check my lipstick as I listen. She wears no makeup, she says, because her husband would never allow her to have it, so she's not used to putting it on anymore. She goes on and on about the relationship...

"So, you say he was abusive and controlling even before you married him?"

She looks down at the table, "Y-yes." She wasn't even sure if she loved him when she married him, but she went through with it anyway.

"So, like, why did you marry him?"

"I dunno. Someone to take care of me, to protect me." And all her friends were married. She was in her early thirties when they met, she said, and wanted to be married before it was "too late."

"Sheesh. Protect you from what? You want protection? Buy a big dog."

She needed to get a job, as she was now destitute because she let her husband control her finances and he spent all her inheritance, mostly on other women she guessed. She suspected all along he was cheating, and now he was leaving her after using up all her money.

"You knew he was up to no good, and you let him handle your money? I mean, there were plenty of warning signs with his behavior, right?"

"I trusted him to do the right thing, and take care of the money for me."

"Why? Why did you trust him?"

"Because... because he was my husband," she broke down into sobs, quivering. "I... I thought he would do the right thing, because he was my husband."

I reach into my purse for a tissue, "I wouldn't marry someone like that."

(Not a work of fiction; based on actual events.)

"Still Got That Magic Touch!"

Ricardo hated his job, he hated the place where he worked, and he hated the people there, also. But it was the only job he could get, and the pay was way too low. He had to lift people, clean up other people's messes, and feed people who would most likely puke up all over on his clean white shirt. He hated everything about his job at Happy Dale Retirement Home.

The commute was also bad, having to drive all the way to Salem, also known as the "Witch City." At least he could laugh at the little old ladies and call them "witches," knowing they might be too deaf too hear, or too senile to know what he was saying.

When the head nurse wasn't watching, he could play a few fun pranks, also. He could spill orange juice all over some old man's pants and then yell, "Oh, I guess yah gotta be changed again, Mr. Jones!" Or tell an old lady her new blue nightgown looked nice, because, "it matched her hair." He sometimes tossed dentures into the dumpster behind the nursing home, also, just so the senile people could not bite him.

It never occurred to Ricardo that the day would come when he himself would be elderly or unable to walk, that one day he might be unable to see clearly or hear correctly, that he may one day become forgetful, or have to live in a facility, forgotten by his own family and left alone to sit and wait for visitors who would never come.

Cindy Lou was suspicious of the new guy. There was just something about him she could not stand. He gave

182

her the creeps, especially when he asked her out. "Leave me alone, Ricardo," she would always say, but he would not leave her alone. He was always in the staff break room, and never around when people needed help. If he wasn't in the break room, he would be out in the back parking lot, smoking. Sometimes he took long lunches and came back smelling like alcohol.

She thought of reporting him, but worried he would do something to get back at her, slash her tires, or worse. It wouldn't be the first time a person's car was vandalized or a purse stolen in that place. She had worked there five years and still couldn't believe that people who worked to take care of elderly people could sometimes be so mean and sneaky. It made her worry about her own parents when they got old someday.

Edna sat and stared blankly at the television in the day room and tried to continue to knit a shawl she was working on. It became difficult as her arthritic hands began to stiffen and ache. She looked sideways as she saw Clyde pull up beside her in his wheelchair, "Edna," he whispered, "Pass it on. Tonight, we go over the wall."

"I don't think you'll make it over the wall, Clyde. Not with your bad back."

"Well, then there's always the tunnel me and the boys have been digging. We could all go out that way, you know."

She just looked at Clyde and smiled. He pretended to be crazy, and he was very good at it.

"And what are we going to do then? Hop on a bus and go to town?"

"Sure. We'll go to town and have a few drinks. I'm buying."

"It's a deal, then."

Then he asked, "Is that rotten, no good orderly going to be working today?"

"Let's find out," she reached into the bag where she kept her yarn and knitting needles and pulled out a pack of tarot cards. She shuffled the cards and pulled one out: *The Devil*. "Yup. He'll be here today."

"How about that nice girl, what's her name? Betty Lou?"

"Her name is Cindy and she's here today, because I saw her walking the halls."

"Good. Maybe she'll find my dentures today. She looked all over yesterday."

"No, I don't think she'll find them. I've a feeling they're gone, Clyde. You'll need to just get new ones."

"Darn it. I shouldn't have to get new ones. I never lost anything until that young punk started here. Things are going missing. Watches, wallets, all kinds of things going missing around here since he started."

"Just let him push too far, Clyde."

"Got something planned, have you, old girl?"

She just looked at him and said nothing. All around them in the day room, other residents of Happy Dale looked away from the television and looked at Edna and Clyde, as if expecting to see something happen. Edna put the tarot cards away and went back to her knitting, "If they would let me use my herbs I could fix this arthritis, you know."

"Can you find my dentures, old girl?"

"No. I told you, they are long gone."

Just then Ricardo shuffled into the day room. He sat in front of the TV and changed the channel to watch cartoons.

"That's my show!" cried Irma, who sat in the back of the room. She actually could not see the TV very well because she was nearly blind, but she wore hearing aids and strained to listen.

"Yeah, old lady? Well, it's my break, and now I wanna see my show!"

"Don't the employees have their own television, in their break room?" said Rochester. No one seemed to know his first name, or if that was his first name, so everyone just called him "Rochester" or "Mr. Rochester." He was a World War Two veteran and claimed to have killed ten—and sometimes he claimed more—Nazis, and three Hitler Youth boys, when he was a younger age than Ricardo.

"Yeah. The other TV is broken, so I'm watching this one, Roger."

"It's Mr. Rochester to you, boy! When I was your age, I machine-gunned twenty Nazis and I don't know how many Hitler Youth! I took a shot at Hitler himself, but I missed, damn it! I would have got him, too, if he hadn't ducked under his Mercedes! Now you just fix that TV back so Irma can watch her soap!"

"Now lookit, grandpa!" Ricardo stood up, towering over Mr. Rochester, and shook his fist, "I've had about as much as I can take from you senile, crazy old people—"

Edna pointed at Ricardo and began to mumble something quietly. She was almost incoherent, but Clyde could still hear well enough to make out a few words like

185

"reprobate," "vermin," and "maggot." Then she closed her eyes and whispered an incantation.

"What? Talkin' to yerself again, old lady?"

And then there was a flash of light and a puff of smoke.

Ricardo suddenly realized he was now very small. He looked up and saw Edna's pink fluffy slippers and the wheels of Clyde's wheelchair above his head. He tried to scream, but all that came out was a faint squeak. He looked down and saw his own legs, all six of them.

"Cindy!" cried Edna, "Cindy! Come here, will you!"

"What is it, Mrs. Johnson?" Cindy Lou came into the day room, wondering what sort of emergency Edna Johnson could be shouting about.

"Look! Look there! Cindy, look at that on the floor!"

"Huh?"

That right there! Cindy, what sort of place is this? I cannot believe, with all the money we pay to reside in this home, that there are cockroaches at Happy Dale! This is supposed to be a top rated home for the elderly, and you have roaches!"

Cindy Lou quickly stepped on the cockroach, "Okay? There! It won't bother you. I'll send the janitor to mop up the spot on the floor, okay, Mrs. Johnson?"

"Thank you, dear."

Edna looked at Clyde again and smiled.

"You still got that magic touch, old girl!" he said.

"I may be old, but I'm still Queen of the Witches."

"Damn! Wish I had my bazooka!" said Rochester.

"That would take him out and put a hole in the damn wall! Take out all the cars in the parking lot, too!"

186

"Shut up, Rochester," snapped Edna, "It's cold outside. We don't want any holes in the wall! You want to blow up a young punk like that, then you need to use sorcery! It's more accurate than one of your stupid guns!"

"And more fun, too," added Clyde.

Irma cackled, "Does anyone know where the TV control is? I hope that fool boy didn't have it in his pocket when the girl stepped on him. We'll never get it back, now."

"They Say She Was a Witch!"

*L*ong ago, and far away . . .

He took her on a bright morning as she went out to milk the cow. Just barely a woman, she knew nothing of men, and didn't even realize what was happening until it was over.

They all told her to keep quiet about it. He was the son of a nobleman, and there was nothing she could do. But she did not listen. She believed she would see the light of justice. And so she went to the authorities. She was brought before the judge. When the young man spoke against her as a witness, he simply said that she had seduced him, and thus she was sentenced to be flogged for the crime of adultery, and then to be tossed into the rat infested dungeon.

Each night in the dungeon was more horrible than the night before. The guards came into her cold cell each and every night and continued to punish her for the crime of adultery, causing her to be an adulteress over and over again.

The rats were her only companions. She shared her meager crusts of bread with the little beasts. Eventually one of the creatures would come when called. It was her only true friend in the world, she knew. But the other prisoners, thieves and scoundrels all, would watch and hiss, "See? She talks to animals! Witch! For sure they'll burn her one day!"

Finally after what seemed an endless sentence, she was to be released from the dungeon. She was brought again before the judge, who ordered that she, as a wicked temptress, should be banished from the village, and from that day must live apart from all good decent people.

A relative took pity upon her, and secretly passed her a few coins, "naturally, dear cousin, you will have the kindness to say nothing of my helping you like this." She agreed, knowing now, after all this time, the value of silence. And so she began to wander away from the village, until near the edge of the dark forest she found an abandoned cottage.

She cleaned it up, made simple repairs the best she could, and there she remained. She kept a few goats, some chickens, and had a garden. One day an old gray cat came by, an unwanted stray like herself; the cat decided to stay. She gave the cat no name, but on a dark night it sat at her feet and purred. She was alone in the cold world, save for her goats, her chickens, and the old gray cat with no name.

An old book was found buried beneath the dirt floor of the abandoned cottage one day while she cleaned and swept. She had little use for it, for like most women, she could not read nor could she even write her own name. She put it on a shelf, and there it remained, unopened. She knew nothing of its importance.

She would go into the village to sell the eggs she collected from her chickens and as she went she would hear the good and decent people whisper, "Adulteress!" "Temptress!" and "Witch!"

The words tormented her, for she knew she was no adulteress. Nothing of her virtue was ever given; it was stolen on that bright morning as she went to milk the cow. And now no one would ever want her; for her hair was now graying, and her clothes had turned to rags. She had suddenly become old, after not more than thirty years in this miserable world.

One day while tending her small herb garden she heard another woman weeping. The cries came from out of the forest. And so she went to find the source of all the sorrow. There, sitting by the woodland stream from which she drew water, was a young woman, her face bloodied and bruised and battered.

"What happened?" she asked. For the first time in her life, she was seeing someone else with troubles possibly as bad as her own.

The strange young women looked up at her, "My husband. I am fleeing my cruel husband. He must never find me! For surely he will kill me!"

"Well, come with me, then, girl," she mumbled, "No one ever visits my lonely cold home."

The girl remained with the old woman for many years, and she became like a daughter to her. She had run from quite a far distance, running for days, stopping once only to drink from a stream. The old woman taught her to cook, sew, and plant a garden. The young girl, when the book was found on the shelf, taught the old woman to read.

"What? You can read?" said the old woman when the girl offered to teach.

"Why, yes. I can read. You've done so much for me, I must do something for you. I grew up in a noble family, and was taught to read and write. But they married me off to a cruel man, and that is how I happened to wander so far from home." The girl flipped through the book. "And this is a strange book. It's a book of potions, spells, and magic. I've never seen such a book, but the good sisters who taught me warned me never to read such things. They say that long ago, many spell casters were found near here and burned along with their books. Where did you get it?"

"I found it, buried under the floor of this house when I came here to be in exile. So now then, teach me," the old woman demanded, after remembering the way she had been treated throughout the years, "Teach me to read so that I may know what is in that book."

And so they learned the contents of the book of magic and spells by the light of the fire each night after the day's work had been done. The old woman, her hair now gray after thirty years of life, learned to make letters in the dirt floor with a twig. She soon learned to write her name, something that most people in the village could never do. One night she showed the young girl how the mice would come to her when she called to them, "A simple trick I learned while in prison for a crime I did not commit. For many years," she said. "The little beasts were my only friends."

"How lonely you must have been," the girl said. She gazed down at the old leather bound book and flipped through the pages. "This page tells of how to curse one's enemies."

"Let me read that passage, then."

In time the plague came upon the village, and nearly all the people died. The two witches, if witches they were, were untouched, perhaps because they lived in exile. And for those in the village who survived, then came famine and drought, the cows went dry, and the crops failed.

"Was it because of us?" The old woman wondered out loud while feeding her chickens. "Is that why all of this happened?"

"I don't know," the girl said, as she hung out the laundry. "I really don't know. Perhaps it was meant to happen that way; perhaps it would happen if we never opened the book. Perhaps it was really the will of God. Or nature. Or perhaps they all just got what they deserved."

"I fear I shall burn in Hell, girl. If I did not commit a crime then, I have committed one now. For surely now I am damned. Or I always was damned. My life has been Hell on Earth. The only good thing that ever happened was having one friend, and learning to read, even if from such a strange and terrible book. No one else that I know can read, save for you, and the man from such a good family who sentenced me to torment and sent me to live away from all the decent good people."

"They all got what they deserved, then."

Many years passed. The old woman sickened and died from a fever one winter. The young girl buried her under the dirt floor where the book was found, and buried the book along with her, so neither would ever be found.

And then she, herself now old, remained alone in the cottage for a while. But then growing lonely and sad, she finally travelled far away where no one knew her and found work as a housekeeper for a wealthy family. She never told of her life with the old woman, whether she was a witch or not. Sometimes while working, she heard the other servants talking about an old witch who lived at the edge of the forest, who was once a wicked temptress when she was young and beautiful, but who lived alone now that she was old and ugly, and who could talk to wild animals, command the rats and mice to dance at her feet, and who emptied an entire village of its people. She never told that the old woman was now dead, that her sorrowful life had ended one cold winter's night.

Present time, somewhere in Western Europe:

The tour bus slowly rolled up to the location, stopped, and let the people out, although many remained on the bus from exhaustion and boredom. They gathered around the ancient site, but all that was left there was the stone chimney and walls beginning to fall down from age and weather. The thatched roof no longer existed, leaving the interior exposed to the sky above.

"And this is where she lived," the tour guide announced. "They say that centuries ago there lived here a genuine sorceress. She could command legions of horrible rats, and brought the plague upon the village, killing everyone, because a handsome young man refused her! Of course he refused her, because she was so ugly! Now we'll be here only for a short while to take pictures, but please don't go into the cottage because it's so old it may be unsafe. Let's all get back on the bus in ten minutes to be at our next stop."

Somewhere in the crowd that surrounded the old ruined building, a child whimpered that he had to pee.

"Was she real?" asked an overweight young American with an expensive camera. He enthusiastically took one photograph after another.

"Of course she was real!" The guide said, "We have historical records going back centuries that show that this

193

woman was sent to live in exile for her crimes shortly before the plague came to take all the lives of the people."

"What crimes did she commit?" The young man asked again, still taking pictures.

"The legend says that she was a temptress, in those days, meaning probably, you know, a prostitute," answered the tour guide, with a sly grin.

"But was she really a witch?" asked a young girl who stood beside the fat American tourist. "Or was she just some poor old lady who was misunderstood? And if she was so ugly, how could she be a temptress?"

"Well," the tour guide smiled, "they say she was a witch."

Suddenly the big American with the expensive camera jumped back, "Oh my God! A rat just ran out of the bushes and came at me! It tried to bite me."

"Are you all right?" asked the girl.

"Yeah, I'm okay! That's weird, though, all this talk about a witch who could talk to rats. The thing almost bit me. Let's get back on the bus. This is a cheap tour. I'm hungry. Let's hurry up; this place is creepy. I think we can get lunch at our next stop."

They Finally Came and Got Him

No one really knew much about Old Man Jenkins. We weren't even really sure if he had a first name, or how old he was. We just all called him Old Man Jenkins. But it's sad that he's gone. We really miss him; he was fun to have around. And we all thought he was crazy, with the way he used to talk.

He'd talk about everything. Like most old people, he was an expert in everything: politics, money, sports, music, cars; but the one thing he never stopped talking about was the aliens.

Old Man Jenkins would sit there with his old yellow dog on the front steps of his old house in the middle of our neighborhood and yell at us kids for making noise. One day our baseball landed right in front of him, but he laughed and threw it back. That's when we started talking to him. Our parents told us to not listen to him too much, because he was crazy, but he was a nice old man once you got to know him. He would invite us in for ice cream sometimes, too.

But if you got him to talk about it, he would always talk about the aliens.

They abducted him once, he said, when he was young. It was the 1960's, and he was young and wanting to travel the world, like most young men did in those days. Nowadays, I suppose most of us don't bother to see the world, since there doesn't seem to be much to see in the world lately that isn't rotten.

He would tell of how he was driving his old '52 Chevy across country, to see America, to drive out to California, and not stop until he would walk on the beach and get his toes into the Pacific. His plan was to either get a good job and stay there, or if he didn't get a job, he would come back home and get a job at his uncle's gas station, learn to fix cars and stuff.

But as his story goes, he only made it half way there. He would park his car off the side of the road at night, pull over, park behind trees so the local sheriff's deputies wouldn't give him a problem, take out his sleeping bag, build a small campfire with whatever he could find, cook some beans, then sleep under the stars all night. In the morning he would stop at a diner for breakfast, then travel on drifting down the road. Sometimes he would stop along the way and work odd jobs for cash, but then move on. I guess that was a young man's dream back then, to get into an old car, take some cash, bring some cans of food, a knife, a sleeping bag, some tools in case the car had a bad day, and put an old guitar in the back seat—and that was all you needed back then.

One night, Young Man Jenkins—because he was not Old Man Jenkins yet—he parked his car in a farmer's field and ate out of a tin can and after playing his guitar to himself and the coyotes, then he got into his sleeping bag to rest peacefully under the night sky, listening to the song of the crickets, drifting off into sleep, and that's when it happened.

That's when They came and took him.

He woke up and there was a bright light, brighter than the sun, but he could look into it and it didn't hurt his eyes. Something landed close by where he slept, shaped like a large metallic disk. We all call them UFO's today, but back then, they called them flying saucers. These

196

small men came down the ramp, that's what he called them, little men, but they were what we call the "Greys" today—he said they were short and skinny with big heads and large dark eyes. They all wore the same skintight black uniforms, no buttons, no zippers, just tight black silk like material, with matching boots. They all marched down the ramp toward him.

Old Jenkins used to tell us how he next woke up on a steel table, with all these horrible, big eyed, strange creatures hovering over him, putting probes into strange places, sticking needles. He used to say how he remembered they took his brain out of his head, looked it over, decided it was probably useless, and then put it back into his head because they decided they didn't want it. Next they removed other parts of Old Jenkins, so that's why he never had any kids. He said they put that back on, too, but it never worked right after they took it off and put it back on. When the aliens removed the probe from up his ass he sat up and screamed and got off the table and ran into a dark corridor, ran down the hall, trying to find his way out.

He went into several rooms trying to find an exit. One room had all these giant insect-like creatures, sitting at a conference table, as if having a meeting. They looked at him and hissed. He kept running and went into another room, and saw all these glass jars filled with what looked like half human, half alien babies suspended in blue liquid. He kept going and came upon some men dressed in military fatigues. One of the men looked at him and asked, "Do you know where we are? Last place we were was Da Nang." He said, "Hell, no, I have no idea where this place is!" One of the soldiers said to the other, "Well, at least we're not getting shot at."

Jenkins kept running until he came upon a video screen that showed the Earth down below. He screamed and kept running until finally a metal door in the corridor opened and a beautiful blonde woman in a long white dress appeared.

"She told me that I had been chosen!" he would say, though he never knew what the hell he had been chosen for. Her name was Princess Alura, and she represented the Star Brothers who came from the Pleiades star system. She ordered the horrible little gray aliens to release him and send him back to Earth, and told him that one day she would return for him in her own ship, and take him away with her to join the Star Brotherhood.

Next Jenkins woke up in the farmer's field, in his sleeping bag, and wondered if it had all been a nightmare. He looked at his watch and realized it was noontime, and got into his car and drove to the nearest town in search of food. He sat at alone at a table in a diner eating blueberry pie and drinking coffee and wondering what it all had meant, and suddenly in front of him was a man dressed all in black: black suit, black tie, black hat, even black sunglasses. He looked at the man in black, "Where did you come from? I didn't see you when I came in."

The man in black sat in the seat opposite him, and said, "You didn't see anything last night. It was all a dream. That's all. It was just a strange dream."

"Yeah? That's good to know. Hey, how did you—?"

But then the man was gone, as if he disintegrated.

So Jenkins got into his car and hit the gas all the way home, only stopping to fill the gas. He did not stop for food, to sleep, anything. He never made it to California. He went home, worked in the gas station around the corner from his house all his life. Never went anywhere else.

We always liked him, when he wasn't yelling at us kids. When he would tell his crazy stories about the aliens; it would make us laugh. The week before he disappeared, he was on his front step with his suitcase next to him.

I pulled my bike over, "Hey, Jenkins, yah goin' somewhere?"

"Yeah. I got this feeling, she's finally gonna come and pick me up."

"Who?"

"Alura. She's finally coming for me. Soon, I think." I was like, "Oh come on, old man, you're crazy."

"She's coming for me. I just know it."

I laughed and rode my bike home. I didn't tell anybody, because we all already knew he was nuts.

But later that night is when it happened. I woke up, and the house was shaking, like as if there was an earthquake. I was real scared. I screamed for my mom, and she didn't answer. I got up and ran down the hall, and my mom was looking out the window. "What the hell is going on?" she said, "Some kind of explosion!"

The shaking stopped, so it wasn't an earthquake. There was just this bright light coming through the windows, without any sound. Then suddenly the light died down. It was all darkness again.

"What the hell is going on?" my mother said again. "This neighborhood has gone crazy. Boy, you get yourself back to bed so you can be in school and make something

199

of yourself so you can get out of this damn neighborhood!"

"Yeah, mom." I went back to bed, but I didn't sleep. I wondered what was going on, too. Mom said there was an explosion, but I didn't hear any loud noise.

I was tired all day in school, and the other kids asked if I was up partying all night. "No," I said. "Anybody know anything about an explosion last night?"

"What you talkin' about, an explosion?" they said. "You crazy?"

"Naw. Never mind."

When I got home I went to see if crazy Jenkins was okay. I don't know why, I guess I just was worried about him. The front door to his house was half opened, so I went in.

"Jenkins? Hey, old man? You there?" But he wasn't there. The house was empty. In the middle of the living room floor was his suitcase. I figure maybe he just went to the grocery store or something, and forgot to lock his door.

Then I saw the man in black, right there, standing in the doorway. He was just like Old Man Jenkins described, black suit, black hat, dark glasses.

"Huh? Who are you?"

"George forgot his suitcase," said the man in black. He came in and picked it up off the living room floor. "I'll just bring it to him."

"His name is George?"

"George Jenkins, yes, that is his name, I believe."

"Where is he? Is he okay?"

"Oh he's fine. He's just going to be travelling. That's all. George says he's always wanted to travel, but he never really got around to it since that last trip he took." He walked out with the suitcase and shut the door behind him.

I went after him, "Hey, mister!" But there was no one there. No one on the front step, no one on the sidewalk, no one on the street, no car driving away. *No one.* So, Old Man Jenkins wasn't crazy after all. Because they finally came and got him!

The Corporation

She awakened to the cold shrieking howl of the sirens, as she did every morning, as everyone did every morning in the gray concrete city. She was having that dream again. She dreamt of a childhood, during a time long ago when people still had childhoods. She dreamt of trees and grass and flowers, a backyard with a dog. That was when people were still allowed to see their families and keep pets.

She crawled out of her bed and into the frigid cold darkness of early dawn. The siren was still blaring. It would stop soon, then start up again fifteen minutes later to prevent anyone in the city from oversleeping. Once she had an alarm clock of her own, one with music, she remembered. But then the Corporation set up the sirens throughout the city to stop tardiness and absenteeism. She quickly showered, ate a small breakfast, left her small one room unit and headed for the elevator, down into the dark lower levels to the subways that ran throughout the city. All the subways led directly to various offices and manufacturing facilities controlled by the Corporation. None of them led out of the city. Once, long ago she was told, people had cars, but the Corporation stopped manufacturing them. So now it was nearly impossible to travel beyond the districts controlled by the Corporation.

The subway stopped at the location where she worked, and so she and many others silently exited and headed directly toward the elevators that would stop at the floors where each person worked. They all wore uniforms with the large black emblem of the Corporation, and each uniform was a different color. There were blues and grays for office personnel, brown or orange for manufacturing, and dark green for maintenance. People who ranked very high in the Corporation did not have to wear the uniform. They dressed as they pleased. But they arrived by private transport, so she very rarely saw anyone who wasn't dressed in the Corporation uniform.

She continued on directly to her workstation, the same workstation she had been assigned to over fifteen years ago. She had long ago grown tired of her assigned department, and had applied more than once for a transfer to a different district simply to break up the monotony of her career, but she had never gotten any response.

The entire work area was dark, with dim lighting. It was more pleasant when they had windows, she remembered. But windows had long ago been banned. Windows were not to be allowed in any part of the facilities controlled the Corporation, except for the uppermost levels. There were never again to be any more windows because of the Incident. It happened long ago, but she still remembered it very well. She had been one of the people involved in the Incident, perhaps that was why she was never allowed her transfer. People still cautiously whispered about it, referring to it as the "Bird Incident." The management simply referred to it as the "Incident."

It started because of Marvin Four Thousand Thirty One. That was his full name, but everyone just called him Marv. Marv was a nice, friendly sort of a person. Before the Incident, she liked to have coffee with Marv sometimes, but then coffee pots were removed. The removal of the coffee pots really had nothing to do with the Incident, it just occurred roughly around the same time, she remembered. She noticed that the coffee pots were gone the morning of the Incident, but was informed by Supervisory Person Seven Thousand One Ninety Nine that they had been taken away the night before. Marvin always liked his coffee, and he seemed on edge because of it. Come to think of it, he had been on edge for quite a while, but now he was really on edge. And then, that's when it happened. Marvin sat near the window. "Look, there's a bird out there," he said suddenly, breaking the dull cold silence. And everyone looked at once to see the bird. There were not many left, and everyone wanted to see it. And that's when someone got up to go to the window to look at the bird more closely. It was Mary Lou Thirteen Fifty Three, who secretly often complained about having to wear the same thing each day when other people higher up got to wear what they wanted to wear. When Mary Lou got up, another person got up, then a third, and then more people. Supervisory Person Seven Thousand One Ninety Nine couldn't stop them or make them go back to their workstations. It took a full ten minutes to get the people to start working again. The bird had flown away, but then someone became fascinated with the red blazing sunset off in a distance, and dared to linger staring at it for a few minutes.

"All of you!" Supervisory Person Seven Thousand One Ninety Nine demanded, "Get back to your computers! We all have a deadline! All of you! Sit down!" Someone hissed something impolite. "Was that you, John One Fifty Three? There are no more birds, John! They have been extinct since the Fourth Decade in the Dominion of Our Great Corporation, and if they're not, they soon will be, so stop looking for them out there. I don't care what you people think you see on that ledge, now go sit down and stay at your computers! You will all remain at your computers until the end of this shift."

She had liked Marv, everyone did. And Mary Lou and John were well-liked by most people in their department. She wondered what happened to them. She got the courage up to ask Supervisory Person Seven Thousand One Ninety Nine about why they never came back, "That is not your concern. Please return to your station and continue your work."

Supervisory Person Seven Thousand One Ninety Nine was not always easy to communicate with. One day when Marvin was still employed by the Corporation, he jokingly called him "Seven Thousand One Ninety Nine."

"You will remember to refer to me as Supervisory Person Seven Thousand One Ninety Nine, please, Marvin."

And so she ceased to ask any questions, or ask for detailed instructions, or even ask if she was doing a good enough job. She no longer knew if she was doing a good enough job for the Corporation, since she no longer asked any questions, because Supervisory Person Seven Thousand One Ninety Nine never communicated any of these things to her. When she was first employed by the Corporation, many years ago, she asked what the work was for and what was its purpose for the good of the Corporation? "You do not need to know that, now please simply continue your work." Mary Lou Thirteen Fifty Three leaned over and whispered that, "Seven Thousand One Ninety Nine doesn't really know what it's for either!

205

And he doesn't care. He doesn't care, why should you?! Why should any of us?"

She agreed but kept silent. No one dared speak against the Corporation, because no one knew what would happen to them if they were no longer employed by the Corporation. There were rumors, however. Rumors about people turned out of their homes, people who could not afford to eat or buy medicine if they got sick, rumors about men and women who existed on the streets, and froze to death in the winter. They were all continually reminded that life would be very, very hard without the benefits of the Corporation. Everyone learned that when they were children.

The Corporation controlled all schools and work training centers, and so all citizens were trained to become employees of the Corporation. In history class, she remembered, she learned that once there were many lesser corporations. But they were all tremendous failures. Then one glorious day the Corporation took them all over and saved all the employees all over the world from terrible layoffs and starvation and chaos and certain doom. Now no one had to go through life wondering what they would do. And no one needed to struggle. The Corporation would take care of everyone, and make all important decisions for them.

The Corporation would decide for people what they would do, where they would live, what they could buy, and life would by simpler and society would run more economically and efficiently. To remind everyone of the continual benefits of the Corporation, all employees would be required to attend training sessions where they would learn more about life outside of the Corporation, and they would then truly come to realize how lucky they all really were to be employed by the Corporation. Of course, she knew it was all true, that no one could live without the benefits of the Corporation. For it was the Corporation that controlled the importation of all foods, the Corporation which provided housing and medical care, the Corporation which now raised everyone's children and provided adequate education and job training. The Corporation provided everything for the world's people. And like everyone else, she was of course grateful for the Corporation.

But sometimes, just sometimes, she had her doubts.

She wondered sometimes about what life really was like outside the Corporation. Were people really starving? Were there really people dying in the streets? She could not know. She only traveled to work and to the small home unit she was assigned to. The doors leading to the outside had long ago been permanently closed, but of course, it was only for safety and security purposes. The Corporation wanted to be certain that all of its employees were physically safe from the unstable elements that were not under the direct control of the Corporation.

"Do you know of the whereabouts of your three co-workers?" She looked up from her computer. It was Supervisory Person Seven Thousand One Ninety Nine.

"No, sir, I do not." She continued to work, but then realized the sudden opportunity, "Would you require any assistance in locating them, sir?"

He looked down at her again and frowned, "Explain?"

"I do not know of their whereabouts. However, I do realize that they have been gone for a time period that is indeed longer than is normally allowed. Would you require any assistance in locating them? Obviously, sir, overseeing the workflow in this department is of much greater importance and would take up too much of your valuable administrative time."

"Yes. Thank you, then. You may assist in the search for your co-workers."

She immediately stood up, but did not thank the Supervisory Person. After all, she was assisting him. An opportunity like this rarely occurred. She could now get up and walk around, drink from the water cooler, check her message bin, maybe travel to the upper levels and see what the people higher up in the Corporation actually looked like. She could move around the vast halls of Corporation Controlled Facility One Thousand Five Hundred and Fifty Nine. It was one of the Corporation's older buildings, and there were closed off areas she had never seen before.

She stopped her aimless wandering when she heard the screams from down the darkened hallway. It came from the old file room. The file room had not been in use since all files were now kept electronically, and the area was basically off limits to all personnel. "No, Steve! Don't do it! Don't!" She heard it again and hurried.

At the end of the long, dark hallway she came upon the abandoned file room, the long ago closed up door was flung wide open, and a bright light glared through the open doorway. It was natural light, the kind she had not seen in a very long time. It could only mean one thing. *Somewhere, beyond that door, there was sunlight, and a window.*

"Steve! Come back in here, right now. You'll fall!" Betsy One Thousand Fifty Nine was nearly hysterical. *"Get back in here, please!"*

"Steve, come on. It's not worth it, okay? Come back in." Joe Five Hundred Forty One tried to stay calm, but it was nearly impossible.

When she walked into the file room, she saw it. There he was, Steve Four Hundred Sixty Eight, at the ledge outside the window, ready to leap to his certain death.

"Why, Steve, why?" She asked when she entered the room.

"How did you know we were here?" Betsy asked. "This is our secret place. No one else is supposed to know about our window!"

"It doesn't matter anymore, Bess," said Joe. *"Steve! Come on. Get in here!"*

"Seven Thousand One Ninety Nine sent me off to hunt you guys down and make you get back to work, that's all. But I won't say anything about the window, or you Steve, either, if you just come back in. Why, Steve, why?"

"Why? Why, she asks! I'll tell you why! Because Stephen T. Johnson, the 'T' meaning Thomas, who is now only known as Stephen, Employee Number Four Hundred and Sixty Eight of Corporation Controlled Facility One Thousand Five Hundred and Fifty Nine, is just not going to take any more of the damned Corporation's shit! That's why! And I don't care if I have to crash land to prove it!"

"Oh Steve, will you just come in here! Think of your wife and children." And now she too was near hysterical. "Steve—"

"My wife? My children? The Corporation hasn't allowed me to see them in years! The kids were all taken when it was time for them to go to school, they took them away to teach them all how to obey Corporate Directives and to perform meaningless tasks! My wife? Don't you three idiots remember? They transferred her out of this facility for spending too much time in the ladies room, and no one seems to know where she is right now. Maybe Corporate Personnel lost track of her documentation. Maybe her documentation is still on some desk, sitting under a ten foot high pile of documentation for other lost people from other separated families! And I, Stephen T. Johnson, the 'T' meaning Thomas, who is now only known as Stephen, Employee Number Four Hundred and Sixty Eight of Corporation Controlled Facility One Thousand Five Hundred and Fifty Nine, cannot deal with any of this anymore! I cannot! I am going to jump—"

"No!" She screamed. But then it was too late. He had flown out into the bright blue and gold day sky and joined the birds, the few remaining that were left. The three of them rushed to the window and looked down, but saw nothing. The building was so tall it was impossible to see him land. His cries of anguish simply faded away to silence.

"What are we going to do now? How will we tell our Supervisory Person?" She worried out loud. "It's not our fault, but he'll blame us, and so will the Corporation. It will be written into our files, and they might transfer us. We might end up doing maintenance or assembly . . ." Her voice weakened and died, and then she realized what she was saying. "Don't misunderstand. I do feel bad about it—"

"We know," Betsy said. "I was thinking the same thing. It's because he's free now, and doesn't have to get up in the morning to perform the same meaningless work anymore. It's like now he can sleep forever, when he finally lands down there. He won't feel anything, maybe. There will just be darkness, like in a dream, and then there will be eternal sleep." She leaned forward to look down.

"Don't Betsy! Don't follow him down there." Joe pulled her back.

"Maybe he's the lucky one, Joe," she said. "Maybe Betsy is right. None of us have any lives. We are just parts of the big devouring machine that makes up the Corporation. His wife will never know. The paperwork will be processed so slowly, it will just never get to her. The kids won't know either. After all, the Corporation wouldn't interfere with their career training by allowing them any time for grief."

"But what shall we tell him?" Joe insisted.

"I . . . I just don't know," she said weakly. "Maybe we can just tell him the truth?"

"No," Betsy snapped. "Then they will board up our window. We'll never see the sun again! Even if it is dangerous, we just can't be without it. I know I can't be without it. It will just be another thing they'll take away from us."

"Then tell him that he sort of . . . well . . . terminated?" she suggested.

"Okay," Joe agreed. "That's it. We'll tell him that then. We'll mourn for him after our shift, but for now, we'll all say that he was terminated. Or, Betsy? What was that they said last year when we lost Jill One Thousand Three

Fifteen? She left to 'pursue other career alternatives.' Then we found her doing janitorial work in the basement. Isn't that what happened, if I remember correctly? I guess it was because she was late more than twice in one year."

"We'll say that, then." Betsy said, "Now, hurry, let's go. Before the Evil One gets worried again and comes and finds us, and has maintenance board up the last window we have in this entire building."

They left to swiftly return to their workstations, but not before they made certain the door to the old file room was shut very tightly.

When the three employees returned to their work area, they were all relieved to discover that their Supervisory Person was on his break. Supervisory People were the only employees that the Corporation permitted to take a short five minute work break, it was part of their expanded benefits. They all sat down quietly and continued their monotonous work. When he returned, he continued on with his sorting of various documentation and rating daily performance. He did not seem to notice the empty seat or question the absence. This was not terribly unusual, since he often did not notice absences when he was preoccupied with other more important tasks. How long would it be, she wondered, before the Supervisory Person finally noticed the absence?

And finally he did. He gazed over toward the empty cubicle. He cleared his throat, "Excuse me, everyone." Together all employees suddenly looked up. "Would any of you happen to know the whereabouts of Steven Four Hundred Sixty Eight? He seems to have been missing from his assigned work area for quite a long time today."

She waited, waited for one of the other two that were involved to speak out. But they did not. She remained silent, and kept her expression blank.

"Oh, I see," said the Supervisory Person. "No one will take the initiative and be pro-active around here. Well, if your fellow employee Steve does not return to his workstation immediately, he may unfortunately face yet another cut back in what's left of his benefits program."

"Cut back? Another cut back? Benefits! Hah!" The sudden roaring scream came from the darkest corner of the department. "Another cut back? Benefits? What benefits!" It was Gerald Two Thousand Five Hundred Forty Six. He had been at his desk longer than anyone, he had been there so long, he even remembered the distant time before people were assigned numbers, the time when people were actually known by their real names. "Benefits? Benefits?" He kept repeating over and over again.

"Is there a problem today, Gerald?" the Supervisory Person walked over toward him and asked the question with his usual mock politeness. "You're supposed to come to me with your problems, you know, Gerald."

That was about all Gerald could take. He had sat at his desk quietly for many years and continued to endure. Today, however, something within him snapped and let loose. She could see him begin to rage far across the distant rows of cubicles. Her eyes were strained and weakened from constant computer use, but she could swear that she saw his face turn red, even at that distance. All of a sudden Gerald stood up, took hold of his computer, and violently threw it at the Supervisory Person. He ducked out of the way too quickly, and Gerald missed him by an inch. "I am sick and tired of dealing with all your shit," Gerald shrieked when the computer landed on the floor. *"You can take your stupid Corporation and shove it up your skinny managerial ass, Seven Thousand One Ninety Nine, or whatever the hell your name is!"*

"What the—?" the Supervisory Person stared in disbelief.

Gerald wasn't listening to the rest of what the Supervisory Person had to say. He got up on his desk and jumped the gray cubicle wall and when he landed he began to run toward the Exit.

Supervisory Person Seven Thousand One Ninety Nine watched along with all the other employees as Gerald ran madly for the door, screaming and yelling about lost benefits and cuts in his paychecks and all the forced overtime. Seven Thousand One Ninety Nine sighed, "I just don't know about the quality of the people they are hiring these days." He looked around the room. *"Continue your work, everyone. We all have a deadline."*

She did as she was told, and continued on with her work.

You Can Really Misjudge People!

I guess I first learned about them on my first night on the job. God, that was a strange night. It was only gonna get stranger, too.

There was talk about it in other precincts, of course. Where I was before, there was talk about "that section of the city." But I thought it was just that. Talk. Stupid talk. Hell, was I wrong. I took the job because I got sick of working the suburbs where nothing ever happens. Now I know that was a dumb move. I should have stayed where I was. Too late for that now.

So I took the job. First night I was there the Sarge comes to me before I hit the road in my cruiser, "Hey, how yah doin'? You know we got a city filled with vampires, right?" No. I didn't know that, I said. I heard rumors, I said. But didn't think. "Yeah," he laughed, "We got 'em. Lot's of 'em! Well, good luck your first night on the job. See yah round!" I was like, what the fuck? I asked around and he wasn't joking. "Yeah," said Rodriguez, "A few in town all right. You'll be workin' the night shift, right? Just stay calm if you meet one, everything will be fine." Then he goes and says, "Hey, just think of them as a pale minority."

I still remember the day this stuff hit the news. Coincidentally, that was my first year as a cop. It was after that awful spring and summer of 2041 when people were dying all over every major city.

Terrorists had finally gone and done it, finally achieved all their crazy Death to America shit. Crazy bastards. Not with stolen jets or with guns or bombs or even poison gas. No. They had to be smart enough to use something we had no way to cope with. They released the Plague, damn it, into almost every major American city. It was Death to America! For real this time. We all were doomed. Scientists and hospitals struggled to keep up. But people were dropping dead in the streets. It spread to the suburbs, to the farming communities, everywhere. We were all going to die.

Then that fall there was suddenly a cure. A cure! Thank God, everyone was so relieved. But where the hell did it come from, all of a sudden? After people began recovering and the dying stopped, the scientist who was credited with inventing the cure called a press conference to announce its source. On TV the guy was so obviously visibly nervous when he began to talk, like he was about to reveal something really heavy. So where did this cure come from? Aliens?

No, not from aliens.

The scientist went on with describing how a group of people contacted him that they were immune to many of the diseases that historically killed off vast numbers of humanity. There was, he said, a race of people living among us and yet had remained hidden from society. And they offered their help. The cure was synthesized by studying their highly evolved immune systems.

Since then books have been written about it, documentaries made. Before, most people didn't believe in them anyway. Now, everyone did. I read a little of the stuff in magazines. Just a little. Never was much interested. Never thought I'd ever meet one, anyway. The ones the magazine found to interview claimed their kind have been hunted and persecuted for centuries. They claimed to buy blood from slaughterhouses, or some even owned cattle ranches and drained it out of livestock, and never harmed people. Naturally, the presented themselves as peace loving and civilized. We helped save the planet, now let us just live in peace.

Yeah, right. I didn't spend my career dealing with drug lords, thugs, rapists, junkies, wife beaters, and the occasional terrorist to believe any of that kind of shit.

The military finally rounded up the terrorists. Took them long enough. What was that they always say about military intelligence? The world was safe now, they said. Not in my opinion, it's not. They were out there.

First night on the job there was a disturbance in this shitty run-down apartment building. A wild party out of control. Neighbors called to complain. I drove around and it was really out of control. Big time. The music was so loud the walls were shaking. This guy answered the door and had a million and a half tattoos, eighty million piercings, purple and green and red hair, fake leather clothes. I thought that went out of style in the twentieth century. I advised him that there had been a complaint and that he should turn down the music. Now. He stuck out his pierced tongue and waved it around like a snake, as if that was somehow cool. Then he shut the door on my face. The music went off, though. He was crazy, but not stupid. He wasn't such a complete idiot that he wanted to risk being tossed away for the night in a cage next to a big guy named Mongo who was feeling sorta lonesome.

Next there was a woman calling because she found her live-in boyfriend molesting her five year old. A bar room brawl. A mugging. Some gang activity. A break-in. It was a busy night. No vampires yet. I was almost disappointed. Nope, I really wasn't. Wondered about the guy with a million piercings, though. What the hell was that? Was it human? Yeah. Probably was. Probably he worked in a warehouse or a mailroom at minimum wage somewhere and spent all his money on hair dye and cheap dope.

When I ran into Rodriguez again I said, "Nope! Didn't arrest any yet!" He laughed and said they tend to be real quiet anyway. "Good," I said. So I hoped.

Another new distraction was this girl who worked the switchboard. God she was beautiful. A head turner. I kept trying to get an excuse to ask her name. I saw her going out to the parking lot at the end of her shift. I figured, this is it. I can find out her name. Yeah, like I could just as easily ask someone, "Hey, yah know the fox at the switchboard?"

So I see her going out to her car. "Can I walk yah out t'your car?"

"That's okay." She had this quiet little girl voice. She didn't even look up at me.

"Gonna walk out with yah, if yah don't mind. Never know what's out there on a dark night."

"Don't worry. I think I know where I'm going. And I don't think I'll trip and fall."

I followed her out, "You're not even worried?"

"About what?" she finally looked at me.

"You know, the vampires."

She laughed. And what the hell was so funny? "Okay, if I see one, I'll let you know." She turned away, still laughing like there was some joke I wasn't in on. Suddenly she turned around, "It's Tiffany."

"What?"

"My name is Tiffany."

"Jeff!" I said. I held out my hand, "You can call me Jeff."

She came back and held my hand, "Jeff," she said, "worry more about the drug pushers and street gangs." Then she left.

Later I figured I should utilize Plan B and ask around about Tiffany. In this way, I could find out if she was married without asking her and looking like a jerk. No she wasn't married. Sometimes her friends thought she had this on and off relationship, but she didn't talk much about it. And she lived in That Part of Town.

Now I was really worried about her safety. I didn't want anything to happen to Tiffany. To be truthful, even if she was ugly I wouldn't want anything to happen to her.

Still I wondered how a girl like her could survive that kind of neighborhood.

I wished I had a partner to go around the city with. It would be safer to have back up. Make the job easier, too. With the population cut in half, there weren't enough people to fill jobs. I drove around and half the places were empty, abandoned. Windows boarded up or broken. Decent looking homes empty. Real sad. The world was recovering, but slowly.

I got home that night and didn't sleep. I just ended up watching this dumb late night talk show. You know the one with this blonde hostess wearing a mini dress walking among the audience taking comments. The Shelby Show. This girl is on TV complaining about her family's reaction to her new significant other. "They just don't seem to like him! The refuse to even get to know him. And he's really a nice guy. He respects me! You know, he waited six months into the relationship before he even tried to bite me."

I wanted to puke out my beer when I heard that. Then this fat dude in the audience gets up and asks, "Hey, I'm Tim from Ohio. Question for Jake? Ah, that girl is pretty hot. Why did you wait all that time to bite her, man?"

Then the guy says, "Well, at that time, I wasn't sure if I wanted to be in a committed relationship."

What in the hell was this world coming to? It's been ten years since the Plague ended. Do we all still have to put up with them?

Then the girl's parents came on. The mother says, "Well, I just don't know about all this. I mean, I don't know if it's right and all. What will the neighbors think?"

The next night there was a complaint about a disturbance in an apartment building. And unluckily enough, it was in that Best Section of Town. The landlord called saying a tenant might have dope in his place, and there was a rumor about weapons. I was like, sheesh. This is gonna be good. This time I had better have back up. Rodriguez came and pulled his car up before I went in. We went first to the landlord. He opened the door and Tiffany was in his apartment with him, along with several other people, men and women and kids, some African-American, some Hispanic, a few Asian, some white, and a few were, I noticed, real pale. Like there was this multicultural crowd hanging around the landlord's place. He told me and Rodriguez that the other tenants were all clustered together because they were scared of their neighbor Bob. So what was up with Bob? Rumors of heroin, coke, meth, guns, bombs, chemical weapons, a few vials of leftover Plague, stuff like that.

Fortunately, Bob was out for the evening. We supposed he went to some hate group meeting, and we hoped he'd be out all night so we could search the place. After all the wars, fortunately the system no longer made you need a warrant, you could just go and bust right in. And we did find evidence.

Let's see if I can remember the whole grocery list correctly. Yeah, he did have coke, heroin, meth. Lots of strange chemicals. Some stuff we contacted both HazMat and the bomb squad about. There were guns—lots of guns. Big ones. Military and terrorist type guns. Scary looking guns, and I've seen plenty in my face. Yeah, some stuff we suspected was some leftover Plague. HazMat picked that up, too. Then we needed to get Animal Control. Bob had a lot of cuddly pets. There was a cobra, a rattlesnake, an alligator, and also something unidentified ran under the couch before we could figure out what the hell it was. He had devil posters all over the walls, which were painted black. Oh, yeah, and there was one more thing. The dude had a stockpile of wooden stakes in the closet. Plus also the same closet, before I forget to mention, there was full of really expensive looking business suits.

The landlord and Tiffany got real upset about that one. And I don't mean the business suits. "Why? Why?" Tiffany kept saying.

"Maybe because I yelled at him for being late with the rent, Tiff," said Mr. Landlord.

This lady kept going on, "That damn fool had alligators in an apartment? How am I supposed to raise my kids with alligators running around, huh?"

The Hispanic guy kept yapping and Rodriguez translated, "He said he would be safer in his own war torn country. But he needs to stay here, because there are no jobs."

This other guy was yelling at the landlord, "How can you let that shithead move in here?" he said. "How was I supposed to know he was planning to blow up the city? He said he was a stockbroker. He looked like a decent person when he signed the lease."

Tiffany said, "Hi Jeff. All the excitement, I forgot to say hi."

I said hi back. Then suddenly I got it.

That was why she worked the night shift.

I couldn't really look at Tiffany in the same way anymore after that. No longer was she like this cute helpless girl I wanted to know, maybe even protect. Now, she was someone I did not want to know. At all. I didn't talk to her anymore, or about her. She ignored me, too. What the hell.

I kind of got addicted to watching that stupid late night show. The hostess had a nice ass, good legs. Yeah. Okay. So call me a chauvinistic jerk. So I like ass. I'm a guy, so I look at ass.

Anyway, this stupid show had on a special for the tenth anniversary of finding a cure for the Plague. First they interviewed people who lost family, whose lives were destroyed by the tragedy. Then they interviewed military personnel who went after the terrorists, some of whom were exposed to the Plague and almost died of it. Last they interviewed test subjects for the medical experiment. I didn't want to hear it, so I got up to shut the damn thing off. But then—and I still to this day cannot believe what I saw—Tiffany was on television right in front of me.

"In order for our immune systems to be able to fight off the Plague, we first had to get the Plague, which meant several nights of misery for all of us. In experiencing the Plague, we built up immunity, then Professor Aubrey was able to synthesize the cure. He tested it on monkeys first. I felt bad for the monkeys, but none of them died, so that was a good thing. It meant hope that they lived. When the animals lived, he said he knew he had it right."

A lady got up and Shelby went over with the microphone. "I just want to thank all of you for what you did for all of us."

The audience applauded. And I really wanted to puke at that. I was at this point getting so damn sick of the whole lot of all of them. The world was now having this sick love affair with these people. Just wait until one of them forgets his manners and bites somebody's little kid.

Then Tiffany smiled and said to the audience, "Well, yes, and I just want to also thank Professor Aubrey. All through it, he was so kind to all of us. He treated us no differently than anyone else. That really meant a lot. Especially to me. A lot of people are still prejudiced in this world, even though things are changing. But it really means so very much to me when someone treats me the same way they would just treat the next person. I mean, it's even really hard for me to come on TV and talk about these things, knowing that people might recognize me now. . . ."

She went on talking, and I felt like a big asshole. Not only was I an asshole for looking over Shelby the Hostess' cute little ass, but I was a really big, super-sized asshole for how I behaved toward Tiffany. Later on during the show—and then I really felt kicked in the stomach—she introduced this guy as her husband. And yah know who that was?

It was the Landlord!

Then the both of them started talking about the trouble they had in society dealing with the way people viewed vampires, and even how one of the tenants in their apartment building was giving them trouble since he was found to have a closet full of scary looking sharp pointed things.

"But to be fair," he said, "the man was also keeping crocodiles and cocaine and a few guns and other odd things like that."

Hey, wait a minute, buddy. He had more than a few guns! In fact, he confessed to wanting to destroy the entire city, plus its surrounding suburbs.

Well, if that's the way he wants to see things, fine. A few guns, my ass.

Later on I ran into the guy who had the million piercings and tattoos. Guess what? The dude is a cop. Yeah, that's right. He was there that night working undercover to bust a drug ring. They figured a dude with fashion sense like that would be perfect for the job. Hey, yah know, you can really misjudge people!

Fatal Heart

Tonight I saw her again, wandering in silently, with more bruises, more scratches, and even a few more bite marks that did not cut deeply enough to cause fatal harm—*yet*.

I saw her drift into her room, and close the door behind her. She did not see me as I stood in the darkened hallway and watched and sighed. I could try to talk to her about it again, but would she listen? I doubted that she would. *Stupid little witch.*

In all my century as a vampiress—*yes, just one century, or slightly more than a century, I'm somewhat young compared to many vampires*—I have seen this tragedy over and over again, with the same violent results: *Death.*

Only this time, it was a witch, and not a mortal woman, rushing into the arms of her own destruction. I thought a witch would know better, but I was wrong. Oh, how wrong I was, thinking a witch would know better than to play with such danger and not know that her own destruction was soon to come.

She reads fortunes. So she should know her own future. Why can she not see her own destruction coming? I have seen many mortal women make the same mistakes and they either die a horrible death, or they live a long time, wishing they would die. Either way, they seal their own fate by following the whims of their own foolish hearts. They choose to remain in what modern people call "bad relationships."

It could be choosing to remain with a drunk, or choosing to remain with a violent reprobate, but somehow, for some reason, they choose to stay.

And many a time I have tried to tell them, get out before it's too late for you. But they never listen to me. It's not like things are the same today the way they were, when I still walked under the sun. Today, it is much easier to walk away from such a mess that one's life has become. And yet, I don't know why so many of them stay?

What draws them all back into danger, even after having broken bones? I do not know. It makes me sad, and yes, I can still feel sad, even though I appear dead cold myself, I still can be moved by—dare I say it? *Pity*.

I have seen this over and over again, as I have said. They are young, they come into town looking for a job, rent a room in my boarding house, and sometimes they meet someone. Usually, if they do, it makes them happy, and their lives turn out well. They stay here for a while, and sometimes they find their happiness.

Sometimes, they find their doom. Sometimes they don't realize things aren't quite right until they wake up in a hospital bed with cracked ribs. And sometimes, after being released from the hospital, sometimes still they return to the one who put them there in the first place. Yes, I thought a witch would know better. But why would she know better? She's still young and foolish. And this time, her great fatal love is a werewolf.

When they first met she would tell me all about how "awesome" he was. I would stare back at her and nod, yes, awesome, right, sure. And you do know he is a lycanthrope, don't you?

"Isn't it like so cool?" she would squeal, and giggle like a child with a new toy.

"Cool? My dear, such liaisons can be rather, you know, hazardous." At the time, I did not tell her that bodies were being found, mutilated, ripped apart, and some even dismembered, in the forests outside of town. Many of us immortals knew about it before the newspapers did, of course.

"You're just jealous!" she whined. "Oh, you are so like jealous!" And she would giggle again. She spun on her spike heel and turned angrily away.

She wanted to be friends at first, because she was an aspiring witch and I'm a vampiress. I'm still not certain who informed her. Another immortal, I suppose, since arriving in town she's been trying to associate with local covens and other beings from the ether. I will find out, eventually. As long as she keeps it to herself, and doesn't tell the other people who rent rooms here. They would probably think she was making it up, or insane. But when I try to give her useful advice, she flies into a childish tantrum.

I put the horrid memory of our enlightening conversation from my mind and retreated to my office to look over the finances for the boarding house I run and to fetch myself a cold bottle out of the small refrigerator I kept far from most people's view.

No, modern vampires don't hunt anymore. We have not for quite some time, actually. Sometimes I would like to, however. I put the container in the microwave and sat alone with my thoughts and looked over my paperwork. A few people late with the rent. Oh well. I knew they would have it paid soon. One of them was a waitress, when she did not get enough tips, the rent could be late. That was Keisha. But she usually came through. The other I did not know what he did for work. Dwayne said he was in "sales." Sometimes he flashed a large quantity of cash, other times he had little to nothing. He drove a nice car. I wondered what he was selling, but he paid his rent most of the time, so I did not bother to ask. And the third resident was a part time telemarketer and part time fortuneteller. Wanda hoped to make it big locally reading tarot cards and such, and eventually open her own fortune telling business. I wished her well. We used to be friends, sort of, until I warned her to worry for her own future.

Now I'm just the "blood sucking landlady." She wouldn't last much longer with that attitude. Just be late with rent a few more times, and give me a reason to send you off. But no. If she did not wake up to her own tragic reality, it would not be me that made sure she would not last much longer, in this boarding house, or any other place. How could she be so blind to what was right in front of her?

I heard the front door creak open downstairs. It was him. He smelled like a pack of wild dogs. I could smell him while I was all the way up on the third floor of my building where I remain during the day. Well, we do have better senses than most creatures. And I could smell blood. Faintly, but I could smell it. It was old, maybe from last night. But it was coming from him. Perhaps he did not bathe often enough. That is a habit of many of these so called wolf-men. That, and their notoriously hot tempers. Some of them learn to control themselves, and some of them need to be destroyed. For that, we—

immortal creatures, that is—we need to call upon the head of whatever pack a werewolf belongs to.

A few weeks ago, I had already made the call. We spoke on the phone. Yes, I keep contact information for almost every other paranormal being in my area—the ones that do communicate—in a small leather bound book that I keep in a place that will never be found. "He is not one of us," Mr. Gray said. "But I will look into it for you."

"Not one of you? Well, is there another pack close by?"

"You know, when I got your voice mail a few nights ago, I made a few calls myself. I am going to ask everyone in my pack. So far no one I've talked to knows anything about this one—*Brian, you say his name is?* I'll check it out for you."

I thanked Mr. Gray, and he said, "Nice to hear from you, as always. I'll let you know if I find out anything."

But he did not call back. And now this stray were-creature was stalking through my boarding house, not only endangering the darn fool girl he had come to visit, but also endangering my few other residents. And me. I did not want to get dismembered, either. That could be very inconvenient. Could take another century, maybe, to grow an arm back after it being ripped off. Nor did I want to clean up any bloody mess or have the police stomping all about after a body was found in my place. If they came here, they might find out what the "salesman" was selling, and go all through my private rooms, and . . . *I did not want to think about it.* Brian the werewolf was wandering around my building, and this was like so not good, as people say today.

Slowly it dawned on me. Perhaps it was Brian who told Wanda about me? Paranormal creatures tend to recognize each other.

I heard him go into Wanda's room. Next I heard Wanda giggling; okay, fine. That will keep him occupied for a while. I hoped. I sat at my desk, trying to clear my head of worry. But next I heard tears coming from Wanda's room on the second floor. Something about not spending enough time with her, and is there someone else? And then he snarled, *"Shut the—"*

And there was someone else approaching. I got up and stepped outside of my small office. Too much information was spread out on my desk. It was Keisha, the waitress, coming up the stairs.

She looked at me, "They're fighting again."

"I know."

"Like, why do you let him come in this house? I mean, the dude is like so intense."

"Wanda is in love, Keisha. There is nothing anyone can do about it, but stand by and watch as the wreckage takes place. Is there something else you wanted to tell me?"

"Oh, yeah. I'll have the rent money tomorrow, okay?"

"Okay, Keisha. That will be fine. Really. Unlike some people, you're quiet and you don't bring trouble."

Downstairs, from the second floor, things got louder.

"Man, he scares me," said Keisha.

"He scares me, too."

"Oh yeah, I almost forgot to tell you. Dwayne got arrested."

"What?"

231

"Yeah. He got picked up selling dope. Hey, you wondered where he got the money, right?"

At least Dwayne wasn't arrested while at my place. "I did wonder, I suppose."

"Oh yeah," said Keisha, before going back downstairs, "Have you read the papers? There was another murder. People are scared there is a serial killer on the loose. They found a dead lady, in a drainage pipe, all ripped apart. Scary, huh?" She went back down the stairs to the second floor where her room was. I heard her shut her door. She locked it.

Yes, it is scary. Even for me, it was scary. I listened. Keisha turned her radio on. Wanda and Brian continued to argue. Dwayne's room was quiet, because it was empty. I had mixed feelings about that. His being in jail meant less rent money coming in. But he was trouble, too. I would rather not have a drug dealer in my house.

Brian stomped out of Wanda's room, snarling obscenities.

"Don't leave me!" she howled, like a female dog in heat. "Don't go!"

"I said not to follow me! Stupid witch."

"Brian! If you keep talking to me like that, you're going to hurt our relationship!"

"What relationship? You're just another piece of meat! Like all the rest!"

"Brian!" She ran after him. I leaned over the railing that surrounded the stairs, looked down, and watched her chase after him.

Keisha's door swung open, and I saw from above that she too watched those lovebirds make their exit from the house. I next heard Keisha complain about not getting much sleep with those two in the house. The great romance of the century, it was not. I sighed, and went back to my work. Soon it would be dawn, and I would rest. And if Wanda didn't come back, well, that was up to her. Maybe she would spend eternity chasing Brian, both of them howling at the night sky together, and the only wilderness that they would fit into would be the local garbage dump. But would she be happy? She would convince herself she was, I suppose. Like a lot of them, she would say she is happy, because no matter how badly Brian treats her, as long as she has Brian, she could say that she was happy. Wanda would be happy with Brian until Brian tore her to shreds.

I looked out the window. Dawn was slowly entering the sky. It was just me and Keisha, dear quiet Keisha, in the house now. No drug dealers or werewolves, or even tarot card readers who pretend to be witches, in my house. I might have a pleasant day's sleep after all. I did not know what I would wake up to, though.

I woke up slowly as the sun left the sky. The house was silent. No fighting, no crying, no screams of passion. I was glad. I could sense only one other in the house, probably Keisha. I got up, began to wander downstairs.

"She never came back." It was Keisha, standing near the doorway with her purse, in her waitress uniform, car keys in her hand and about to leave for work. "I don't know where she is. It's you know, I saw in the paper, they found another body in the woods. They don't know who it is yet. It's a girl, but the cops can't identify. Do you think we should be worried? About Wanda, I mean?"

"Worried? Maybe. But there isn't much we can do, Keisha," I said. "You know, it's her life. So if she wants to ruin it, she can do that all by herself." Yes, I was worried.

"They were so loud last night, fighting, you know," she said. "I gotta go. Oh, yeah, I forgot. The cops were by and they were asking questions about Dwayne."

Then she was out the door.

I said goodbye and knew she was right. She was only twenty-one, and she was right. We should be worried. And there was nothing we could do.

And I didn't know if Dwayne would be coming back, either. I looked out the window and saw that his BMW was gone. He was probably released, told to appear in court, and then decided to just disappear. I could search his room, but probably would not find anything. If he had anything illegal, I hoped he was smart enough to take it with him when he left.

Maybe I should search Wanda's room, instead? Why not? So I went to look through her things, maybe to get a clue as to whether she'd be back, or more likely to try and understand her better.

She had various frivolous things scattered around her room. So-called New Age crystals, which were supposed to be magical but actually just a recent fad; a Ouija board, her tarot cards—all thrown around her unmade bed and not in order, of course—several odd books about witchcraft, not the ancient books of sorcery. No, these were nonsense books you'd get in the New Age section of the bookstore. I picked one up, "Secrets to Love Spells." The cover said, "Attract exciting lovers from all walks of life!" The author described herself as the head of a coven and relationship expert. I rolled my eyes and sighed even though there was no one to hear me. I tossed the book back into the pile of her assorted things that I considered garbage. I looked around her chaotic room and saw that there were statues of Hindu gods, peacock feathers, her cheap makeup, and more books. I picked up another, "Relationship Repair: How to fix your broken relationship." But I did not see anything I did not know already: that she fancied herself a mistress of the occult and was obsessed with finding love. She did not seem to know it takes many years to learn occult skills and it takes hard work and maturity. Nor did she know the difference between having love and having a death wish, it seemed to me.

The front door bell rang. I wondered who it could be, since I was not expecting anyone, and the people who rent rooms all have their own keys. I went down to the front door, opened it, and there before me, was a policeman. *Oh, terrific,* "Yes, officer?"

"Excuse me, ma'am, I'd like to ask a few questions."

"Well, what about?" I pretended I did not know, but I could guess.

"About a young lady named Wanda Johnson. This was her last known address?"

"Yes, she rented a room here. Why? Is there trouble?" I thought he would ask about Dwayne.

"She's dead, ma'am."

"Dead?" I was expecting something would happen to her eventually, but still I was shocked. It was rather sudden. I half expected the foolish girl to come home all upset with Brian again. "All I can tell you is that she was in a bad relationship with a troubled young man by the name of Brian. I really don't know his last name, but they had an argument last night. He walked out the door and she went after him. She hasn't been back, officer. And that's all I know. I don't even know his last name. It's tragic, but I'm not really that surprised."

"Do you know if Brian had been physically abusive?"

"I believe so. I warned her that he didn't seem good for her, but she would not listen. She ran out the door chasing him last night, and that's probably the end of her sad story." Of course, I could not tell the policeman she was a witch and that Brian was a werewolf and she was probably trying to tame him with a love spell and it didn't work so he tore her apart and they won't live happily ever after. "I'm sorry, officer, that's all I can tell you."

"Your name, ma'am, for the record?"

"Rachel Moroy."

"Thank you, ma'am."

"Thank you, officer, I hope you get this troubled man off the streets." But I knew, they probably would not find him.

Just then Keisha's car was coming back and she parked on the street in front of the house as usual, got out, then saw the police officer.

"Keisha," I said, as she came up the front walk, "Do you know Brian's last name?"

"Huh? Brian's last name? I think Wanda said it was Lobo, or something like that. What happened?" She handed me an envelope, which I knew was the rent, finally.

"Wanda is dead, Keisha," I said. "And Lobo sounds like a made up name to me."

"Oh my God," she was shocked, as if neither of us expected it, "Well, that's what she said his name was."

"I know, Keisha. A man like him will say a lot of things that aren't true, Officer," I said. "Where was she found?"

"At the edge of Route 152, ma'am, heading west." He went on to explain that it was believed she was killed somewhere else, and was possibly shoved out of a car as it went on its way down the road, out of town. He would not give any more details, and I really didn't want to hear anymore.

"Oh my God," Keisha cried, "I knew he was bad news."

The officer began to question Keisha, and I went back up to the third floor to my office and shut the door. I picked up the phone to leave a message for Mr. Gray, but he answered.

"There's been an incident," I said. "A serious incident. Can we talk?"

"Meet me where we usually meet. Tonight, at midnight."

"I'll be there."

The cemetery was quiet and I was thankful. Sometimes at night it can be filled with teenagers who are doing drugs, making out, or pretending to perform some arcane ritual, or some other activity their parents would not approve of. Also there are occasional vagrants that inhabit the place from time to time, before travelling on. I walked quietly through the graveyard until I came to the edge where the old cemetery met the forest. Gray shadowy forms of several wolves ghosted through the woods, emerging from behind trees and bushes. I heard a low growl, then a lupine whimper. I looked around. There he was, in human form, sitting on a headstone. He lit a cigarette.

"I gotta quit this habit," he said. "They say nothing can kill us, but I don't know."

"It's kind of you to meet with me, Mr. Gray."

"Nice to see you again, Miss Moroy. I actually wanted to call you again, you know, about the person you asked me about. It seems he was actually travelling through. He tried to join up with another pack in the next town over, but they wouldn't have him. They smelled death on him, and called me and warned me to tell my pack to have nothing to do with him. Then I remembered the stuff going on in the paper. I figured it could be him. I sent two of my best werewolves to go find him and tell him he can't stay around here if he was going to make trouble."

"So? Was he willing to leave?"

"No. I had to go take care of it myself, tell him to get the hell out of my pack's territory and get out of town. I asked him if he knew anything about the bodies they found. He said no. I figured he was lying."

I was now trying to put together what happened. Brian was told to leave the area. He didn't want Wanda to go with him. She wanted to follow him. So she did. She got into his car, they argued again, and he killed her and tossed her onto the road, "Well, another life has been taken by him, Mr. Gray."

"We're awful sorry we couldn't take care of it sooner. You know, stuff like this makes us all look bad. It's terrible, isn't it? Too many incidents like this, people start wondering if we actually do exist after all. Well, it was nice to see you, but I've got to run. Full moon, you know, stuff like that." He dropped his cigarette, stepped on it to put it out, went down on all fours, transformed, and followed the other wolves into the forest.

"Thank you again," I said. I was glad Brian was gone, but he would only reappear somewhere else, and be someone else's problem, or kill again.

I looked across the darkness of the graveyard, stared into the night, and I was sad. Wanda had ability, some natural talent, and she could have made something of herself. She could have had a future. She could have created her own magic in this world. She existed in this realm of existence for only a short time, and now she was gone, as if she never lived at all. I gazed into the night mist and wondered if her spirit wandered out there, somewhere. I wondered if her soul was finally free, or if her ghost still wandered the Earth, searching endlessly for Brian.

Off in a distance, I heard a mournful howl.

Hit and Run

Cliff shuffled slowly into the classroom with Fenris following along behind him. Both were bored. They were bored with school, and with their classes, and already they were bored with their new teacher Ms. Thompson. They shuffled in and sat down.

"Settle down, class, settle down!"

Cliff and Fenris looked at each other. Her insistence that they all settle down only made everyone throw more papers, talk louder, fight more intensely.

"I said settle down! Ladies and gentlemen, will you please!"

Cliff whispered something nearly inaudible.

"Yeah, sure. Come on over around six. Mom says we're having lamb, again, as usual—"

"I said be quiet!" she screamed.

Fenris sighed, "Hey, like, we weren't being that loud, okay?"

"Settle down!"

He moaned and began to say something to Cliff, who was laughing.

"That is enough! We do not need that kind of attitude from you, young man! Now! Today, class, we are going to discuss—"

"Attitude? Wha—?"

"Fenris! That is enough!"

"Shit," he whispered.

Cliff snickered, and began tearing paper out of his notebook to create a really excellent spitball.

"I'm talking to you as well, Clifford!"

He put the spitball in his pocket to save it for later.

"Now. Today we will talk about multiculturalism!" Suddenly her voice was filled with enthusiasm. "Multiculturalism, class, is—"

Cindy raised her hand but didn't wait to speak, "Excuse me, Ms. Thompson, but we know all about that already!"

Cliff nodded, "Hey. Yeah. Like, that ain't nothin' new!"

"Settle down right now, Clifford. Yes, just about everyone in our society, even some of the people in this town, by now, has heard of the tremendous importance of multiculturalism!" she sounded as if she had rehearsed, "But, the question some of you may wish to ask is, why do we need to know anything about multiculturalism?"

"Yeah!" Fenris didn't bother to raise his hand, "What the hell do we need this stuff for anyway?"

"Well, Mr. Lupin, since you so strongly insist on knowing why we need this, it is simply because of the extremely isolated and backward rural area in which you young people unfortunately live. If any of you young people become, somehow, extremely lucky enough to break away from this type of stifling cultural isolation and go out into the real world, and go on to a higher education, you will need to learn to deal with different kinds of persons! Does everyone understand?" Ms. Thompson looked around to see the young confused faces, "Any more questions? Class?"

Cliff was the first to speak up, "We don't really need this stuff, Ms. Thompson."

"And why not, Clifford?"

"Like, we already know about how to get along with different kinds of people."

"Clifford!" She grew even more frustrated, "What on earth could you possibly mean?"

"Cliff's right, Ms. Thompson," Fenris said quietly, "Even around here, there's different kinds of people."

"Y-yes," she still did not understand. "Everywhere we go, some people are short, some people are fat, some people are bald, but—"

"Ms. Thompson—"

"What is it now, Fenris!"

"You're new in town. Maybe you won't understand what we mean. But you see none of us really need—"

"That's enough Fenris. Now, if, *if*," and she stressed the word if, "if any of you escape this, this vast empty tract of farmland, and go on to a university, you may encounter persons of different cultures, persons with different values, persons of foreign lands—"

"You're the foreigner, lady!" Fenris stood up and stormed out.

The late afternoon sun warmed the meadow while the cool winds blew through the tall grass. Fenris gazed sadly at the empty blackened soil before him. He dropped to the cold ground, sat in the grass, and looked down at it. Even though the flames had burned away decades ago, the field and flowers had never grown back into it.

He looked up when he heard footsteps.

"Hey. We were wondering where you went!"

If was Cliff. And Cindy. She was following him through the woods.

"Hi." He said simply.

"Like, is this where—" Cindy shut herself up quickly. She shouldn't have even said it.

242

"Yeah," he answered.

"Oh my God."

"What's a matter, Cin?" Cliff sat beside Fenris and wasn't really expecting an answer.

"Then it really happened."

"Yeah, Cindy," Fenris said. "It happened."

She sat down beside Cliff, "Like, I thought it was just something people talked about."

"No." Fenris continued to look directly forward down into the blackness.

"How long ago was it?"

"I dunno, like, 1954, or something, I guess."

"Was he related to you?" Then she felt stupid. He had to be, of course.

"He was my grandfather. My Dad was just a baby when he died. It seems so long ago, but people still think about it a lot."

"Did they really shoot him?" she asked.

"Cindy, shut up, will yah?" Cliff was irritated, "Leave him alone."

"It's okay. Yeah. They shot him. And then the family cremated him. Right here. But when they shot him, then they saw what they did, and saw who they really killed, and then they all felt bad. It's real stupid to talk about this stuff any way." He went silent.

"Then the good repentant townspeople all swore never to shoot at another wolf ever again!" Cliff felt compelled to finish the legend. He laughed. Then he too went silent.

Fenris stood up, "Come on. It's gettin' late."

"You trying out for the track team this year?" Cliff followed along.

"Nope," Fenris said.

"Why not?" Cindy asked.

"Because it's just too damn easy, that's why not." And it was true. He naturally outran everyone. It was just too damn easy. "Mom says we're having lamb again. I'm sick of it."

"Hey, your parents own the biggest sheep ranch around. So what else should they have?"

"Yeah? Just once I'd like to go for a pizza and a beer."

After supper Cindy left to walk home early and complained that her parents didn't want her staying out late.

The woods were cool and dark but not empty. The forest was filled with the sounds of life, the cry of an owl, the song of the crickets, the crack of the twigs under their running feet.

They arrived into the meadow and finally Cliff could see with the light of the moon and the stars. He found a stick and tossed it into the air laughing, "Here Fenris! Here boy!"

Fenris ignored him and dashed swiftly across the field.

"Hey, wait for me!"

Ms. Thompson pressed down harder on the accelerator of her Toyota minivan. She was returning from a late night teacher's meeting, hurrying home in disgust. Some of the parents felt upset when she proposed to pass out free condoms and also present a series of lectures on alternative lifestyles. When one mother protested that it was up to parents to bring up their children, not her, she could not take it anymore.

Young minds, she felt, should never be repressed by outdated belief systems or medieval superstitions, and she had never seen a town so completely buried under superstition as this. The outrageous things she overheard in everyday conversation, and the ridiculous things these farmers believed in.

She could stand it no longer! As soon as the divorce with her anthropologist husband was finalized, she would head straight back to New York City where she belonged. It was his fault, after all. It was his insane idea to come out to the middle of nowhere to study newly discovered ancient Native American artifacts. She wasn't concerned. She had a good team of lawyers to help clean him out. Not that he really had anything of any value besides his antiques and old books.

A dark gray shadow rushed into the middle of the night blackened road. She hit the brakes fast and hard.

Too late!

Oh well.

What was it?

A raccoon? No. Too big. Must have been a stray dog.

She put the minivan in park and got out, hoping there was no damage to her new Toyota.

"Oh my God! No!" The scream tore out of Cliff's lungs, leaving the bitter taste of rage and terror in his dry mouth. "No!" He ran out of the woods and into the street.

He looked down and heard Fenris whimper. Fenris raised his gray muzzle in the harsh glare of the headlights, his eyes blood red with helpless sudden pain.

"Cliff? Is that you?" It was Ms. Thompson, walking out around to the front of her car, high heels clicking against the cold pavement, "Sorry about your dog, Cliff. It's hard to lose a pet," she spoke with her usual passionless dry monotone. "Perhaps you could take some time out of class tomorrow to talk out your feelings with the school counselor, Mr. Hinkel."

He looked at her in the semi-darkness. That was all she said, that was all she cared to say.

"Y-you . . . you killed him."

Fenris moaned again.

"Look, Cliff. I know it's very difficult. But he's almost gone. Euthanasia is the best thing in this situation. Surely there must be a vet, even in this location."

"Y-you . . . you . . . you bitch!" He couldn't stop it. And he had never spoken that way to anyone before.

"Why, Cliff, I hardly think that this situation calls for—"

And then a very human cry of pain called out into the night's darkness, Fenris whispered Cliff's name, coughed, turned over and spit up blood onto the pavement.

Ms. Thompson looked down again, gasped in horror and stepped quickly back.

"Oh God—" It was a word she almost never used. She did not believe in God, nor did she want to start believing in any superstition of that sort now. "Cliff? I thought. I thought I saw . . ."

"You killed him," Cliff sobbed. "He was my best friend, and . . . and you killed him!"

"Wasn't there a big gray dog here just a moment ago? Cliff?"

Fenris looked up at Cliff, then gazed vacantly up at the stars in the cold quiet black velvet sky for a long, silent moment. He closed his eyes and was still.

246

"You're a murderer. . . . You—"

A snarl echoed from the darkness of the forest that surrounded the desolate road. Then another. Shadowy gray-black forms drifted through the trees. Two sets of fierce green eyes emerged from the woods.

Strangely, she felt somehow relieved. Even though she could now be mauled by some rabid feral animal, or worse—sued for vehicular homicide, she felt relieved, "See? There is a dog around here—"

"No, there are two of them, and they are his parents, Ms. Thompson."

"What?"

A tall elegant blonde woman emerged from the darkness, dressed much the same way most of the townsfolk dressed: jeans, denim and flannel barn coat, and heavy suede work shoes. She wore her straight shoulder length golden hair simply. But something about her seemed . . . different.

"We knew . . . we felt it." She said.

From behind her came her husband, he walked out of the woods and onto the dark cold pavement. He was of average height, average build with dark brown hair. There was nothing extraordinary about him, yet the look in his eyes chilled her. He gazed coldly right into her, right through her. "What you have done is completely unforgivable."

"Ah . . . " she hesitated, thought about what she would say, "Okay, there's been a little incident here—"

"Little?" the woman said coldly.

Cliff whispered something.

"Cliff here tells me you're the Lupins. Mr. and Mrs. Lupin! We haven't met, have we? I'm sorry about this, really. I—"

"We want you to leave town," said Mrs. Lupin, "Immediately."

"What? Don't you want to fill out a report at the police station? This town does have a police station, doesn't it? Look, we have got to follow the proper procedure here—"

"Leaving town now would be the best thing for you to do. Send for your personal things later, have someone come get them for you," said Mr. Lupin. "We mean this very seriously."

Ms. Thompson grew irritated, "Look, people! This is the twenty-first century. There are proper procedures for dealing with these situations. I have a cellular phone. I can offer to call the proper local authorities for you. I can also offer to assist you two in finding counseling services."

"No!" Mrs. Lupin demanded. "Just leave. We'll bury him ourselves."

She stifled a sudden laugh, "This is not the good old days, okay? There are public health laws, in case you don't realize it—"

"In the good old days, you would have been torn to shreds by us and the rest of the pack, which is what you truly deserve." A long, drawn out and mournful howl cried out from the far distance. Then another, "They are on their way, and they felt it too. They all know what you have just done to him."

"What are you two village idiots talking about?"

Cliff finally broke his silence, "They're wolves! And you just killed their cub! And you better just get outta here or—"

"Why Cliff, I thought you were intelligent!"

"Shut up," Mrs. Lupin snarled. "Get back in your car, back up off of my son's broken body, and head down that road and do not stop driving, or when they come we will let them have you, and there will be nothing left of you except for a few scraps of bloodied clothing littering the pavement."

"Forget her. Let's go," said her husband. And he bent to pick up his son's limp body. "Come on, we'll bury him, and leave her here to her fate. She has earned it."

Mrs. Lupin followed behind him as he drifted back into the forest, "Come on, Cliff. It's okay. He would want you to come with us. I know he would."

Cliff hesitated a moment, "B-but—"

"Don't wait here, Cliff."

He followed them into the woods.

"You people really need a lot of help!" Ms. Thompson screamed as they left, "I know this is a stressful time for you all, but please, it's really in your best interest—"

A snarl echoed behind her. Then another.

She did not turn to look. She retreated to the minivan, slammed the door shut, and locked it; her shaking hands reached for the ignition to start the engine.

A series of furious howls followed her as she sped hysterically down the dark country road.

"So Then, Yah Had a Good Day!"

The overweight acne-faced kid with the tremendously spaced out look was staring at my legs again. I started to blame myself for wearing this skirt. I should have known that if I were dumb enough to wear this skirt that some strange spaced-out teenager would stare at me all during the entire ride on the bus. I stared back at him. He pretended not to know why I was glaring at him, and he twitched, looked the other way, and then when he thought I was ignoring him, he started staring again. He was completely turned around, leaning over the back of the vinyl seat, with his mouth hanging wide open.

Finally he got off, along with the elderly lady behind me with the clattering dentures who kept mumbling to herself. I was alone on the bus, except for the driver and the constant whine of the diesel engine.

The entire day had been a freaking nightmare.

As soon as I walked in the door the CEO stalked up to me and cornered me against the wall and began to interrogate me. He did this to someone each week, it was just my turn. He asked, "Who had left the boxes of trash in the hallway outside the cubicles?" It took me a full fifteen or twenty minutes to convince him that they were not my boxes, it was not my trash, and I really did not have any idea in freezing cold hell who had left them there.

After a while, he left me alone, and I began to think. The janitor, who often lifted the petty cash at night—he worked late, who else could have left them there? After all, wasn't leaving trash around his job? Yeah, I figured, they had to be his boxes of garbage.

Later in the morning the production manager had an emotional breakdown and took a hysterical fit aimed at the art director, who happened to be at the coffee pot near the front reception area where my desk was. It created lovely background music for screening calls from potential clients.

During my coffee break, the Vice President, who was recently married to a girl about my age, ordered me into his office to take a letter, but instead he began to fire off a round of questions about my nonexistent personal life, "Come on, baby, we all know that something's going on with you and that bookkeeper! You can tell me," he smiled horrifyingly, "We're friends, aren't we, honey?"

At lunch my best friend at the company told me about her husband's problem. He took her bonus money, which she was saving for Christmas, to buy his dope. So her mother, who lives on a small pension, gave her the money she needed so her kids could still believe there really was a Santa.

The rest of the day just sucked. I did so many spreadsheets my eyes burned then fell out of my head and landed on the keyboard. The CEO, recovered from his worrying about the garbage, which I will still insist was not mine, demanded I type a 49-page proposal, and he needed it within twenty minutes. One of the things I always liked about him was that he was so reasonable. The office manager drifted out of her cubicle to tell me she was depressed because she worked at this place, which she accurately described as being a pit.

So I took a ride home on the city bus because my car was in the shop. I figured a bus ride would be the easiest part of my day. Right?

Wrong.

Then this strange guy got on the bus. Now I was no longer alone. He looked like he weighed 600 pounds. "Hey, man," he sat beside the bus driver. "How yah been?"

"Fine. How you been?" They made small talk, then I heard, "Hey, man, look at that back there. Let's go have some fun!" "What you talkin' about?" "Her, you and me, let's go back there and get some fun. Let's go, man! This is our chance!" "No, don't do that," the driver said quietly. "Why not?" "Forget about it. Just let it go. Your stop is coming up soon anyway. You'll miss your stop."

He finally got off at his stop. Oh my God. I was so relieved.

The bus driver was glaring at me through the rearview mirror, "Hey, you! Come up here! Sit here, up front."

So I did. Then I just simply said, "Yeah?"

I wanted to pretend I didn't really hear what I thought I heard.

"Did yah have a good day?" he asked.

"No. I had a lousy day! Okay? I had a lousy hell of a day!"

"Oh yeah? Look down there, look down, look down out the window. Tell me what you see down there."

We were crossing the river over one of the city's many bridges, "What do yah see?" he said again.

"The bridge!"

"Do yah know there's people that live down there?"

"No. I didn't know that. How come they live there?"

"Cause they got no job. Do you got a job?"

"Yeah," I did, unfortunately, "Yeah, I got a job."

"Are you livin' under a bridge?"

"No!"

"So, then yah had a good day!"

I looked down again, and I realized he was right. No, I didn't live under the bridge, and I didn't get hijacked all the way to hell in the back of the bus, I wasn't homeless, or on crack, or any of the other things that afflicted so many people in this fine city. And for all I knew, the bus driver probably just saved my life.

"Yeah, you're right. You know that? You're right. I had a good day."

(Based on actual events.)

About the Author

Rose Titus exists somewhere in cold, dreary New England, with two manipulative cats and a very out of date Macintosh with which she creates horror and fantasy fiction. She also has a restored classic car to ride around while in search of adventure.

For travel she has stayed for the night in an allegedly haunted castle, has taken a boat ride on Loch Ness, and has visited the fabled Bermuda Triangle without getting lost.

Her work has previously appeared in *Lost Worlds*, *Lynx Eye*, *Bog Gob*, *Mausoleum*, *Midnight Times*, *Blood Moon Rising Magazine*, *The Bugle*, *Weird Terrain*, *Descend*, *Wicked Wheels*, *Carnival of Aces*, *The Dead River Review*, *Fortean Times*, and other literary magazines. Her novella *Night Home*, her novels *After Dark* and *All the Way to the Moon*, and her collection of short stories *Key 13* have been published with Hypothesis Press and are widely available.

When she's not writing or messing around with her old Buick, she waits by her mailbox for the next issue of *Fortean Times* to arrive.